MOONLIGHT
CLAIMED
MIYO HUNTER

MOONLIGHT CLAIMED

MIYO HUNTER

This one's for Esther.
Sushi and ice-cream with you gives me life.

CONTENT WARNINGS

This book contains:
    Graphic depictions of violence.
    Mature sexual situations.

If you object to violent imagery, cursing and spicy scenes, this is not the series for you.

-xoxo Miyo

CHAPTER 1

KIRA

S o you might be wondering how I got here... panting. Sated. Covered in the cum of my worst enemy.

Would you believe me if I told you it all started with a silly little masked ball?

THE MASKED BALL was *not* the highest social event of the year. That honor went to the Winter Solstice ball. Nothing epitomized the power of the wolf like a party on the longest night of the year.

In comparison, the Masked ball was just for fun. There was even a prize for any shifter who could successfully hide their identity until the end of the night. But it still meant that I was subjected to hours of fittings, decisions over dress cuts, and selecting a mask. It was tedious and neither I nor my wolf had any patience for it.

Of course, in order to be a true masked event, the ball attendees were encouraged to mask more than just their faces. The use of strong scents, like clove, mint, lime and bergamot were enough to hide identities even from our heightened wolf senses. With all the mixed scents, my wolf might come out of this with a headache, but it was worth it for the excitement of the night.

I was running late. There was barely enough time to fix my hair and struggle into my dress on my own.

This time, it wasn't even my fault. I helped Professor Sandoval move the telescopes after his Advanced Astrology class. Everyone was in a rush to get ready for the dance and more than half the class just left the equipment out. Professor Sandoval wasn't a young man anymore; I couldn't leave him to move everything back on his own.

But now I was dashing through the castle hallways like a hot mess right before the party. As everyone else was rushing to finish their own preparations for the ball, there was barely anyone around to see me. If I was lucky, there wouldn't be anyone to even—

I skidded to a halt, and barely avoided crashing straight into someone as I rushed around the corner. Quickly, I opened my mouth to apologize, but snapped it shut as soon as I recognized who I'd almost run down.

It was Magnus Grimson.

Magnus glared at me like I was a scrawny and weird little insect swimming in his morning porridge.

I hated him more than anyone; I don't even know how hating him had started, maybe it was hatred born on sight. Like the opposite of love at first sight. Maybe it was born out of the feud that he held with my older brother Sylas. Magnus and Sylas were always competing at school. I'd heard way too many conversations at the dinner table about how Sylas planned to crush him. But more often than not, Magnus ended up besting my brother in both hunting competitions and exam scores. After defeat, instead of conversation, Sylas would go quiet and broody at dinnertime. I don't know how it started, but from the first moment that Magnus and I met, we were destined to be enemies.

We were oil and water. Peanut butter and asparagus. The two of us had entirely the *wrong* energy. Whenever we got too close to each other, I could feel it simmering and festering in the surrounding air. He noticed too, that clashing tension between us, though Magnus never deigned to even mention it.

"Watch it." He made the words sound like a threat, with menace dripping down each syllable.

Oh, right.

I forgot the most obvious reason Magnus Grimson was on my shit list. More than anyone else, he was the world's biggest and rudest jerk.

I barely even spoke to him, and he acted like I was poison just for existing. Even while running through the hallways I gave him a wide berth, preferring not to risk brushing past him.

Whatever. I didn't have time for the hatred and disdain coming from Magnus Grimson. I had a masked ball to get ready for.

IT NEVER WOULD HAVE HAPPENED if I wasn't thrown off by all the scents in the castle. I wasn't clumsy, and with my wolf at my side, I was a killing machine. I was lethal, with all the grace of a predator... but that was before I was shuffled into this tight ballroom, and overwhelmed with competing masking scents of hundreds of attendees. It wasn't just the scents of shifters wafting all over the ballroom. Humans also attended this little soiree, and they had no idea how intense all these scents could be. They just loaded on the perfume.

Within me, my wolf was sulking. She had her little paws pressed to her nose as if that would do anything to cover up the horrendous cacophony of scents in the air suffocating her.

With one shaky hand, I grabbed myself a flute of champagne—something to soothe my nerves. The drink was sultry on my tongue, with a crisp flavor made sweeter by the soft caress of bubbles. It went down easy, and after a minute I could feel the alcohol numb some of the anxiety in my wolf, easing me into the flow of the party. As my wolf's senses faded and the overwhelming smells became muted, the colors grew brighter.

The dresses of the party-goers took on a shining life of their own, the decor a new vibrancy. Snatches of conversation grew less distinct as they faded into background noise, like the burbling of a river, like music hovering in the wind.

When my wolf was ascendant in my mind, I would have been able to make out each word in the conversations around me. Even now, the scents were loud on my delicate nostrils, like everyone was shouting them at me. Without a bit of alcohol, this party would have been too much to handle. I noticed I wasn't the only wolf in the crowd reaching for another drink and knocking it down the hatch.

The rush of the crowd, the swish and sway of ball gowns, the snug fit on my royal blue A-line dress, the corset pulled tight against my chest... everything was too much. I felt overstimulated and realized that I'd downed my two drinks too fast, and they were a little stronger than what I was used to. The room began to lurch as all the fancy gowns and suits, scents and conversations, pressed in *too* close, crowding my mind. I just needed a minute. Just needed... one second just to *breathe*.

I pushed back away from the dancing crowd, slinking as far from the others as I could. It was too hot in here, too stuffy with all the scents mingling in the air, and the alcohol rushing through my veins. I pulled off my elbow length cotton gloves. The fabric was too coarse against my overheated skin. Pulling away from everyone, I walked backwards, into a corner of the room partially blocked by a vertical column.

Straight into a wall... it took me a minute to recognize it as a wall of muscle.

Oh, damn it.

I jerked away and almost tripped on my kitten heels. I would have fallen, if it wasn't for his large hand grasping my shoulder to help me steady myself.

One finger brushed against my bare skin—that one touch changed *everything*.

Swirling blue light ignited, directly under the spot where he held me. The light swept across my shoulder in a pattern of constellations and lunar positions that burned into my skin, marking me permanently.

Though I knew exactly what I would see, I glanced at his hands. A tattoo burned across his palm... the pattern was an exact match for mine.

That wasn't just any man I'd bumped into. This mark

where we'd touched was a sign that came directly from the moon goddess… It meant that he was my soulmate.

My throat went bone dry as I tried to swallow nervously. I turned around slowly to see who fate had decided was the other half of my soul.

Even with the dark mask over his eyes hiding half his face, I could immediately feel it. All the way down to my bones, I knew—he was everything I never knew I wanted. My soulmate towered over me, his gray eyes peering into mine as his pupils darkened with desire. His nostrils flared as he leaned closer, taking me in. Luckily, the two of us were already on the outskirts of the party, partially hidden by an ornate set of roman columns, or the flash of light from our soulbond would have attracted the attention of the entire party.

His deep voice sounded strained with tension as he murmured, "come with me."

He led me completely out of the ballroom and down the hall. He pulled me far from the other party go-ers until it felt like I had walked halfway across the whole castle. His hold on my wrist was unbreakable. Irresistible. I would have followed him anywhere.

As soon as the two of us were alone, my soulmate stepped closer, backing me up until I was right against a wall. I had nowhere to go and nowhere I'd rather be. His eyes were drawing paths down my body that sent a chill down the full length of my spine.

Even through the harsh scent of clove he'd used, I could pick up the strong scent of his arousal building in the air around us. I'd already decided that it was the best scent I'd ever encountered.

It was like he couldn't help himself… or maybe I was the one who couldn't help myself. All I knew was that I was irresistibly pulled into his orbit. Drawn in by the dark need in his eyes.

Fuck.

I'd been waiting for this. It was as if everything in my entire life had led to just this moment.

My lips parted. I was completely under his spell. There was magic thrumming between us, something more than just the mark of the goddess that had newly emerged on our skin.

He moved even closer until he was flush against me and I could feel his erection pressing up against my stomach. He wrapped his arms around me. All I knew was that nothing felt more right in my entire life than the slow trails his hands traced across my body.

He sunk his fingers into my hair, holding me in place as he kissed me.

His lips moved harshly against mine, and I melted into his touch. He slanted his head, pushing me harder against the wall, demanding something I was all too ready to give him. I parted my lips, allowing him in.

Goddess, my mate could kiss.

He tasted like the sweetness of champagne and the dark thrill of the unknown. He tasted like a hunger I could feel echoed deep in my core as his tongue danced desperately against mine. The caress of his tongue, that sweet friction, awakened a hunger in me that I was powerless to fight against.

I wanted to drown in his taste, in his touch. More than anything, I just wanted *more.*

The way he moved his lips against mine felt just right, and I moaned softly into his mouth.

He broke the kiss, breathing harshly, before pressing hot, open-mouthed kisses down my neck, lighting my entire body up. His touch became hungrier, jerking me against him sharply, as if he was barely holding on to control. He stroked along the underside of my breasts and down my stomach, as if he needed to get his hands on every inch of me.

A growl reverberated deep within his chest that was more beast than man.

I shuddered as desire bloomed in my lower belly, tense with need. There was nothing left of me but a pit of aching emptiness and I needed him to fill it. I parted my legs, needing him closer. Needing all these blasted clothes out of my way. I rocked my hips against him, seeking just a little more friction.

The way my body responded to his snapped the little bit of control my soulmate was hanging on to.

With a strangled groan, he lifted my skirt, parting my thighs wider as he reached between them. Pushing my underwear to the side, he slid a finger into my pussy. I gasped at the feel of his rough finger plunging inside of me, much thicker than my own.

His head dropped to my breast, teasing my nipple with his teeth through the silky fabric of my gown, until the friction had me writhing against him, squirming. On the edge and desperate for something to push me over.

I was dripping for him. I could feel my wetness sliding down my thighs, as he pushed a second finger inside me, grinding the heel of his palm against my clit until it was throbbing. He thrust his fingers into me faster until the tension within me burst all at once. The walls of my pussy throbbed against his fingers as I came. I tilted my head back, letting out a high-pitched cry, as my orgasm ripped all the way through my body. Waves of bliss thrummed through me, reducing me to my wild, animalistic need for pleasure.

I heard the rustle of his belt, as my soulmate freed himself, and his cock sprung free. I felt him right *there*, prodding at my entrance.

He held himself back, gazing at me.

I swallowed down my nerves as I nodded.

Yes.

I wanted him. If I couldn't have him, all of this tension was going to rip me apart.

Thankfully, he didn't make me wait.

My soulmate slotted himself against my entrance, and with a little push, he was inside me. He thrust into me, and I winced as I felt a pinch somewhere deep inside myself. Sliding deep, he pressed until his hips were flush against mine.

My breaths were ragged as I forced myself to relax, to adjust to this new version of myself who fucked their soul-mate before even taking the time to learn his name.

"That's it, you've got all of me." He murmured.

My soulmate seemed to know, without me having to tell him, that I'd been a virgin. He held himself still, though he was vibrating with tension, as he forced himself to hold back the beast within. His wolf must be desperate to claim me.

Once my breathing evened out, he pressed his lips to mine hungrily, keeping his lips locked against mine as he began to move.

His rhythm was gentle at first. Each stroke into me was slow, though it hit so deep I could feel him all the way into my stomach. But he quickly lost control over his steady pace. His grip clasped tight enough on my hips to leave bruises, as he used his hold on me to grind me closer against him after each hard thrust.

It was so intense. I couldn't think, not with this delicious friction making me completely lose control. My eyes snapped shut as I savored the sensation of his hot cock moving inside of me. Feeling each delicious slide of his hardness within me.

"Eyes on me, Darling." His voice was familiar, but so hoarse with lust that I couldn't place it.

My eyes snapped open and locked on his dark eyes that were burning with hunger. His eyes were the only part of his upper face not completely hidden by his mask. Even half out of my mind with lust, those eyes stirred something in my memory.

My soulmate snapped his hips against mine hard, and I shuddered.

He felt so damn *good*.

I widened my legs, taking him deeper, welcoming each hard thrust as his cock slammed into me, over and over.

"You take me so well." His praise stroked the fire within me higher.

I wanted this. Wanted him to slam into me faster. Wanted him to force me to take it until I was stripped of everything human and reduced to nothing more than primal instincts.

My soulmate's thrusts became frantic as he lost his rhythm completely. He pounded into me faster, his pace turned brutal, like he was trying to lose himself in me. He let out a groan that was low and masculine and sent a shiver down the entire length of my spine.

With one sharp thrust, he stilled, grinding his hips insistently against mine. Within me, I could feel his cock pulsing, and the warm rush of his cum filling me.

I clutched at him as I caught my breath.

His lips crashed into mine hungrily, and his hands slipped into the curls of my hair, accidentally dislodging my mask as he deepened the kiss. The clatter as my mask fell to the floor was jarring enough that I broke away from the addictive taste of him.

When my soulmate got a clear view of me without my mask, he went very still.

"Kira?" His deep voice sounded strangled, as if my face set off the trigger mechanism to a cruel trap.

No.

That voice. I know that voice.

It couldn't be true. I reached up with shaking hands, pulling off my soulmate's mask.

Reality came crashing down on me.

My fated mate. The man who was the other half of my soul... was *Magnus Grimson?*

This was not happening.

I had to be dreaming. I had to get out of here. Because it couldn't be Magnus. It couldn't be true that my soulmate was a man who made it clear in every word he spoke to me that he hated me.

No.

Fate couldn't be so cruel. I did not just discover that *Magnus fucking Grimson* was my soulmate, someone who was *disgusted* by me. Not now, when he was still inside of me, right after he'd flooded me with jets of hot cum.

I'd given him my virginity.

Even if Magnus hated me, his wolf wouldn't take that lightly. The wolf wasn't going to ever let me go. He was going to think that I was *his.* That he'd claimed me and that was the end of that.

I would never submit to being the mate of a man who treated me the way Magnus had.

Magnus' mouth was wide open as he gaped at me like a fish on land.

His cock was still hard inside me. His cum was currently dripping down my thigh.

I was so fucked.

CHAPTER 2

MAGNUS

For my entire life, I was only dead sure about two things: that I had a wolf lurking under my skin and that I wanted Kira Valdis.

Kira.

From the first moment I saw her, I craved her. Her scent was my drug, lighting my skin on fire, as my desire for her boiled in my blood.

I'd never had to fight against myself harder than I had fought my compulsion to take Kira and make her mine.

I knew myself well enough to know that if I gave in and pursued her, I would never be able to stop.

Wars had started among the shifters over wolves who had taken mates for themselves. If a wolf had claimed another's soulmate and refused to give up their chosen mate after the soulbond sparked... that was the gravest insult to their soulmate. It was an abomination.

If I ever let myself have a taste of her, I knew that I would never be able to give her up. I would start wars to keep her, fate be damned.

So I did the only thing I could; I pushed her away. I

never allowed myself close to the temptation in Kira's curves, or the scent coming off her skin that drove me wild. I resigned myself to waiting for my soulmate.

I told myself that I would give Kira up. I wouldn't stand between her and the shifter that fate had chosen for her. Though at night I dreamed of letting my wolf out to play, hunting down her soulmate, shredding through his stomach and removing each one of his organs.

I'd hoped that I would want my soulmate, even a fraction of the amount that I had longed for Kira, even though I could never really see myself with anyone else. Honestly, the thought of any other woman vaguely repulsed me, tightening my stomach into knots. It was always Kira's face in my mind as I pleasured myself, her name on the tip of my tongue after every climax.

For one brief moment, when I was fucking my soulmate, I thought to myself that it had all been worth it. Pushing Kira away had been the right fucking thing to do, because there couldn't be any pleasure more exquisite than the way that tight pussy gripped my cock. I had wanted my soulmate. Desperately. I hadn't even bothered to learn her name. I was so consumed by the overwhelming need to get her away from everyone else and make her mine. Get my scent on her so deeply that no one else would ever touch her.

Of course, it was Kira all along. How could my soulmate be anyone else? It had *always* been her.

That had all come crashing down the second that she'd pulled my mask away. The second Kira saw that *I* was her soulmate, she froze as if she was the prey and I was some monster set on mauling her.

I never thought that I would have to second guess my decision to push her away. Apparently, I had done it too well. Being with her was the single most intense bliss I'd ever felt, but as soon as she saw my face, the *second* that my soulmate recognized me; every inch of her body had tensed up as her eyes widened in horror.

I pulled out of Kira gently, my gaze locked on the trickle of my cum that leaked out of her. I wanted to push it back inside of her. I wanted to smear it into her scent glands. Instead, I let it drip to the floor, uselessly. Even through the harsh scent of clove, I caught the scent of the riot of emotions building within her, a bitter mix of panic and fear.

Kira wasted no time in adjusting her dress, smoothing out the wrinkles as if that could wipe away everything we'd just done. She moved away from me, slightly, as if that little bit of distance could lessen the bond forged in our very souls.

"This was obviously a mistake." Kira muttered, looking away from me as she tried to hide the tears forming in the corner of her eyes.

I grit my teeth, and said nothing. Obviously, mistakes had been made, but they were my own. It was my mistake to misinterpret my desire for her.

Even before the coming of age ceremony where my wolf burst through my human skin revealing himself, I had always felt him. I'd known it better than I'd known my own name, that he was there waiting for me. Why hadn't I recognized the bone deep desire for Kira for what it was?

What the fuck had I done?

I had to fix this.

"I don't care if you want someone else. We don't need to be together." Kira crossed her arms defensively, as if she was bracing herself from my rejection.

What?

Did Kira think that I had pushed her away because I had a chosen mate?

"No." The air was still heavy with sex and our scents mingled together. "There isn't anyone else."

Her eyes, which were usually deep blue and lovely, went fierce with determination. She took a deep and shaky breath to steady herself. "I reject you."

My wolf, who had been on the verge of sleeping, fully sated from claiming his mate, awoke instantly. Within my body, he jumped to his feet, hackles raised. He was fully ready to tear apart this threat to his mate, pausing in confusion when all he saw was Kira before us.

I closed the small distance that had formed between the two of us. Even that small space was too much now that Kira was trying to pull away from me. I backed her up against the wall where I'd slid into her tight pussy only minutes ago.

"You're rejecting me now? After you let me fuck you?"

There was a hint of raw fear in her eyes, brimming under her cold mask of indifference. Kira brushed her tears away ruthlessly, tilting her chin to meet my gaze. She faced the barely constrained rage of the beast within me without flinching.

What a brave little wolf.

"I never would have let you touch me if I had known it was you." Her voice was stone cold. I could hear in it, an echo from every time I had brutally pushed her away. Kira was so sweet and lovely, and had never once deserved any of the awful things I'd said to her. She deserved better than me. It was just too bad for her I was a selfish bastard.

I would never be able to get the sound of her soft moans out of my mind. I would never forget the blinding tightness of her pussy clenching around me. Never.

I would not give her up without a fight. Even if it was *her* that I would have to fight, I was never going to be able to give her up.

Kira thought that she was able to reject me?

She was mine.

"My wolf doesn't acknowledge your rejection and neither do I."

Leaning in, I pressed even closer to her. Kira went tense as she felt me grow hard once more. The tighter I tried to hold Kira to me, the sharper and more acidic the scent of her fear burst across the air.

Within me, my wolf snarled. Not at my mate, but at *me*. I could sense his anger at me. My wolf didn't like the way I was treating her. He couldn't stomach the scent of her fear.

I wasn't going to be able to convince Kira tonight. Without saying another word, I stepped back. She pulled away from me, frantically, as if she was desperate to get free. Kira tore down the hallways, as if she was running for her life, as if she was terrified that I would hunt her down.

I let her go. She needed some space to come around to the idea that everything was different. She had a soulmate now. The only reason my wolf allowed it at all was because my scent was all over her. Any wolf who got anywhere near her would know how thoroughly I'd marked her with my cum—she was drenched in it.

I could let her go. For now.

If any male touched her, if they even looked at her the wrong way, I would kill them.

Kira Valdis was *mine*.

CHAPTER 3

KIRA

I jammed my head beneath my pillow, as if the downy feathers could be enough to stop the glare of the sun or to block out my heightened wolf's senses that heard each insistent thud as someone pounded against my bedroom door.

If there was ever a day that I deserved to sleep in, it was this day.

"Any particular reason why Magnus Grimson is prowling outside of your room? Or why he nearly tore out my throat when I tried to come in?" My brother asked through the doorway.

I jammed the pillow harder against my face as I groaned. Maybe if I pressed it hard enough against my face, it would make me pass out and I'd wake up to find that this was all some kind of weird dream.

My brother wouldn't let up, pounding against the door hard enough that my wolf began to stir, putting her on edge.

Ughh. I pulled myself up, not bothering to check in the

mirror or throw something on over my pajamas, before wrenching the door to my room open.

"Goddess, what the fuck happened?" My brother drew back, appalled before stepping into my room to get a closer look at me.

I blinked wearily at Sylas, not awake enough for this.

Well, maybe I should have done something to my face. I don't know, washed it or something? As if that was going to be enough to make it look as if I hadn't been up half the night crying. I hadn't bothered to wash off my makeup or take out the hairpins last night. I probably looked like a disaster. But whatever. *I* wasn't the one charging into my sibling's room stupidly early in the morning and demanding answers.

Wordlessly, I pulled up my sleeve all the way to my shoulder, exposing the soulmark newly branded into my skin.

I couldn't say the words out loud. Admitting it out loud made everything too much, when nothing seemed real. How could any of this be real? How could this be happening to me?

"You and Magnus?" Sylas looked up at me sharply. Saying his name out loud shattered any illusions I built for myself.

I didn't say a word, instead I stared into a corner of the room, willing myself not to cry. *Again.*

My eyes stung from the tears I'd already shed.

Maybe I should go talk to Magnus now. I was sure that my puffy eyes could kill off any tentative feelings my ill-fated soulmate might think that he had for me.

"The moon goddess must have made a mistake. Magnus hates me."

"What did he do to you?" Sylas' expression grew cold as

the scent of his anger flooded my room with acidic spikes of cortisol.

I shook my head. It wasn't like he had forced me to do anything that I hadn't enthusiastically consented to. It didn't help that the sex had been phenomenal. Mind blowing even, until I realized that it was with him. Why did I have to enjoy sex with him? It was as if my own body had decided to betray me.

"It wasn't anything he did. But Magnus is just so cruel to me. He always has been." I thought I was all out of tears, but they came trickling down once more and I couldn't do a single thing to stop them. "I just don't understand it. I guess I'd always assumed that the moon goddess would send me a mate who would love me. Instead, I got Magnus Grimson."

Sylas' wary expression didn't waver at all. Neither did the cloud of adrenaline that flooded the room. "You know that among the wolves, Magnus has a sort of reputation..."

It didn't surprise me at all that Magnus was a wolf with a reputation. Whenever someone said that, it meant that the wolf in question was too violent, and that people should avoid them for their own safety. The rest of the pack would turn a blind eye if a promising wolf was too aggressive. They usually ended up as generals in the war, if they didn't end up mauling too many people.

"What kind of reputation?" I didn't really want to know, but I asked anyway.

"People were always talking about his wolf's instincts. There's something not normal about them. He's in tune with his beast to a degree that people have always found uncanny. There's no hesitation from him. It takes most people years to sync with their wolves. There's usually some disconnect between man and beast out in the field, but Magnus never had that."

"So he's got killer instincts? Is that all?" I was muttering like a petty child and I didn't even care. I did not want to sit here and listen to my brother practically worshiping the talent of the man I didn't want as my mate.

"I've competed with him for long enough to realize that if he was an average wolf, I would have beaten him at some point. He's not."

I had no idea what point my brother was trying to make. Why did he think it was a good idea to tell me that my mate wasn't normal? That did nothing to change the fact that I didn't want him.

"I rejected him." Or at least I *tried* to.

How he took that rejection wasn't my problem. I didn't want anything to do with Magnus Grimson. End of discussion.

"You rejected him?" Sylas raised one skeptical eyebrow. "Then why is his smell all over you?"

I flushed bright red, refusing to meet my brother's harsh gaze. "I might have had sex with him. But that was before I knew who he was."

"You were willing to have sex with a total stranger and now you're mad it's someone you know?" Sylas did not sound impressed with me. "How did your wolf react to you rejecting him?"

My wolf had been dead silent. I could feel her fiery anger. She clearly thought that I was being stupid about this, that I would have to come around to accepting him.

"She's going to have to get used to it." I muttered.

"He's an asshole. But his wolf is going to tear him apart if you reject him." Sylas cocked his head at me, in a wolf-like gesture, as if he was trying to allow his wolf to see me more clearly.

"Well, that's his problem. Not mine." I crossed my arms over my chest. I knew my lupine history, and I knew my rights. While it might not be common, it wasn't unheard of for wolves to reject their soulmates under extreme circumstances. I would say that a lifetime of bullying and mistreatment from the man clearly qualified as grounds for ignoring the soulbond.

"Magnus isn't the only one who is going to challenge this. People around here don't tend to accept when someone denies the soulbond. There are plenty of wolves still waiting to find their mate. Frankly, they are going to absolutely despise you for finding yours and turning him away. They will shun you. That isn't something that your wolf will be able to handle. Isolation and rejection are hard on a pack animal."

I couldn't afford to be rejected. Not by the entire pack.

Sylas and I had been orphaned quite young, so the threat of abandonment was all too familiar. I barely even remembered my parents; I only had vague images of their faces, and I wasn't even sure if those were quite right. But what I did know for certain, was that my life had plunged straight into uncertainty once they were gone.

I knew how wrong it felt to be shuffled around. I knew what it was like to be watched over by people who did not want me. Though I had Sylas, and he'd always shielded me from the worst of it, I knew exactly how devastating it was to abruptly lose everything.

One day my brother and I sat at the high beta table, surrounded by all of our friends. Then without notice, we had our meals all the way at the back table, with the old gamma wolves. Friends wouldn't make eye contact with me any more, classmates wouldn't respond when I tried to talk to them in class, as if I'd suddenly, inexplicably, gone invisible.

Our closest relative willing to take us in was the woman we called Aunt Beau, who was really a second cousin, and rather neglectful in her old age. She was a low-ranking wolf, and my brother and I were left to face the harsh readjustment as our social hierarchy shifted to the rank of our new guardian.

Is that what Sylas was getting at? Was I risking complete social annihilation if I turned my back on a higher-ranking mate?

So what was he expecting me to do? Endure being Magnus' emotional punching bag for the rest of my life? Why? Just so the pack that barely acknowledged me now wouldn't *completely* shun me?

"Why are you on everyone else's side about this, instead of mine? Why won't you just listen to me?" Each consonant I uttered was sharp. I was on the verge of fucking screaming. Not even my own brother was on my side with this.

"Kira, you can't mess around with the soulbond." Sylas shook his head slowly.

I knew that. I spent my entire life preparing for my soulmate. I'd never dated anyone, and barely even flirted. All I'd ever done was wait for my soulmate, like a good little wolf. I listened to all the promises that I would find the shifter who was the other half of my soul, specially chosen for me by fate and the moon goddess herself.

I never thought that I would regret it.

I would have fucked around, and let myself live it up if I'd known who fate had in mind for me.

"Don't talk to me like I'm not treating this seriously." I scowled at Sylas.

"Have you ever considered that he might treat you differently now that he knows you're his mate?" Sylas' eyes flashed golden, as his wolf ascended within him, as if he was trying to reach me through his primal instincts. He spoke with the wolf's soft howl, trying to pull at the pack bond within me, to get me to understand the motives of a fellow wolf.

I shook my head.

It didn't matter. That wouldn't take away all the damage that Magnus had already done. It wouldn't erase the way he had already treated me.

"Even if you wanted to break the bond with him, this isn't the way to do it. He's prowling out there right now. People are going to start talking, if they aren't already."

Sylas was being obnoxious, but he had a point. I was never going to figure out how to end this amicably by hiding in my bedroom, simply pretending that Magnus Grimson didn't exist.

I pointed at my door, signaling for Sylas to leave. I was about to just kick him out for all the good that he was doing me right now. But his last words gave me another idea.

"Fine. Tell him to come in."

CHAPTER 4
KIRA

Magnus Grimson's presence was larger than the four corners of my bedroom could contain. His scent, dark and musky, filled every square inch of my room the moment that he stepped over the threshold. I was going to have to scrub all of my furniture with bleach to get his heavy masculine scent out of everything. Why was this my life, that Magnus Grimson was walking into *my* room, *my* safe space where I slept, like he had any right at all to be here?

He walked toward me slowly, with the careful measured gait of a hunter, as if he was the predator and I was his prey, ready to bolt. His gaze was heated and locked on mine, watching me like he wanted to devour me.

I was sitting on my bed, as it was one of the only places to do so in my room, but I regretted it the moment that he approached. Magnus Grimson towered over me. The dark waves of his hair fell across his sharp gray eyes as he looked down at me.

I ignored the obnoxious part of me that whispered. *Dark. Tall. Handsome.*

Goddess, no. I ruthlessly shoved that thought way far down, deep into the crevices in my mind where I could smother it.

As he leaned in closer to me, my body reacted.

I could feel heat pooling in my core as a shiver ran down the full length of my spine. I cut my next breath short, because if I hadn't, it would have ended up as a harsh shudder. My pussy was a fucking traitor, who did *not* get the memo that Magnus Grimson was bad news. This was the man who had hurt me more than anyone else in my entire life. He should *not* be the man who was making me wet.

Why did it have to be *him*?

Magnus kept his face carefully blank, even though he had to be able to smell my arousal in the air, which slowly grew thicker. No matter how hard I tried, nothing made it fade. My body did not remember the time when I nearly bumped into him after my Alpha politics class and he snarled at me like he was rabid—like he actually wanted to hurt me. Nor did my body seem to remember any of the countless times that I had crossed paths with Magnus, only to have him curse and treat me like my existence was the worst kind of poison.

No. My body didn't care.

All my body could remember was how rough his hands felt against my hips. How his cock slammed into me, punishingly hard. How he was possessing me, dominating me with each sharp thrust. How Magnus made me feel so fucking good.

My clit was aching, desperate for friction, and my panties were drenched.

Damn it. Fucking damn it all.

Now Magnus seemed to be leaning in, drawn to the

thickening brew of pheromones that were coating the air like a fog.

He was too close, his presence was too strong and too masculine, and he was looking at my lips like he wanted to kiss me.

This was all just too much.

"I will never be your mate." I forced myself to say the words out loud, needing to put some space between us.

He blinked as if I had jostled him out of his own thoughts.

"Confident words, considering I had you coming apart on my cock yesterday."

Magnus was staring at me with an offensively proprietary look in his eyes, looking over every inch of my body as if he was recounting exactly what it felt like when he was inside of me.

"I am never going to let you touch me again." I leaned away from him, regretting it when I realized that all I was doing was angling myself closer to my mattress.

Magnus was closely watching my every move, and his pupils darkened, as if he was imagining pushing me down the rest of the way until the both of us were lying flat on the bed.

"No? I think that I'm going to have you begging for me. Begging for the pleasure that only I can give you."

I shook my head, trying to knock the pretty picture that he was painting with his words out of my head. Magnus thought that I was going to be *begging* him? Did he imagine in his twisted fantasies that I would be on my knees groveling and desperate for him, after all the shit he had put me through over the years?

"You're fucking crazy."

"I'm the crazy one? Are you telling me that you can't

feel this? You can't smell the attraction in the air? It's so thick I can taste your desire, even when you're pretending that you don't want me. You're fighting a losing battle against nature. The two of us were meant for each other."

"I will never be yours."

"You're already mine."

I wanted to deny it again, but found my gaze lingering on Magnus' palm, at the constellations and moon phases that fate had burned into his skin. I couldn't take my eyes off his rough hands, where he had left his soulmark out, and proudly on display.

Magnus leaned closer until his lips were at the shell of my ear. "One day you are going to give yourself over to me completely, and I will take care of you and worship you like the goddess you are."

He spoke quietly and confidently as he poured his poison into my ears.

Who in the gods' earth was this man, who was whispering all these dark promises?

Where was the Magnus I had known for my entire life, who had always made me feel like the lowest and dirtiest scum?

The words of my brother echoed in my mind. *Isolation and rejection are hard on a pack animal.*

How would the others react if the weakest Valdis orphan rejected one of their high-ranking wolves? It wasn't hard to imagine the whole Stonevalley pack growing cold, turning their backs on me if I rejected my mate, for what they would see as no reason at all.

Was I ready to deal with the fallout? Could I handle being ostracized, forced to start my life over again?

I had already lost everything in my life once. I could do it again.

But what about Sylas? What would my public shunning do to my brother?

Aunt Beau could do nothing to shield him. If I went down, would I drag my brother down with me? He was my only living relative. Was I about to screw up what he'd been able to salvage of his reputation?

More than humans, we were hard-wired for connection, our wolves were not meant to be alone.

Magnus was lingering near me, watching my every move with unwavering attention.

If he wasn't Magnus... would I be so determined to drive him away?

No.

The answer was instant, and the moment I thought it, I knew it was the truth. If Magnus was anyone else, I would be lapping up all of his attention. His masculine presence, the heat of his strong body so close to mine. It all felt so good. Too good...

What if I tried to see him like he was a stranger? Just start over with Magnus completely. For Sylas' sake. If Magnus was anything like the asshole he'd always been to me, I'd have all the justification I needed to leave him.

This was Magnus Grimson—he was bound to fuck things up.

"I'll give you one chance. But if you hurt me again, you will never get another."

As my words registered, Magnus' eyes darkened, and he took in a sharp breath.

The last thing I expected was for Magnus' plush lips to come crashing down on mine.

CHAPTER 5
MAGNUS

I was fully expecting Kira to slap me across the face.

Instead, I kissed her, hard. Kira's lips were stiff with surprise that quickly softened as she melted against me. As I moved my mouth against hers, demanding more, Kira gave in, letting me deepen the kiss. Letting me have her, though I did nothing to deserve it.

I should have given her time. I could sense Kira's confliction, the storm within herself as she fought against her need to have me and the need to push me away.

The gentlemanly thing to do would have been to give her time to come to terms with everything. To give her soft words and let her see how *good* the two of us could be together.

But my wolf could sense that Kira was pulling away from him, and he was desperate. On the brink of going feral. Frantic to renew our claim on her in the only way that he knew how.

I leaned my weight against Kira, bearing down until she was flat against her bed. Never had I felt so out of control, as if I was watching myself walk headfirst into disaster and not being able to do a single thing to stop myself. I kissed her desperately. Like this was the only chance that I had, like my entire life had endured for this one perfect moment where I got to taste her sweet lips, and feel all of her soft curves beneath me.

I was going to stop—this had already spiraled out of control. I'd already taken things too far. But then... Kira moaned beneath my lips.

Hearing her cry out in pleasure made me lose whatever was left of my mind. All of a sudden, I was feeling along the hem of Kira's thin pajama top. I slid my hands just under the fabric, feeling the impossibly silky skin of her belly. I brushed a trail up her torso until my thumbs stroked against the underside of her breasts.

I had to see them. I would fucking die if I didn't see them.

With one sharp tear, I ripped the thin material of Kira's shirt, yanking it apart and exposing her.

Something short circuited in my brain when I saw her bare and perfect form. One second I was looking at her rosy nipples and the next I had my mouth on them, my tongue swirling all around the perky bud. No conscious thought made. I was magnetically drawn to her. Sucking rhythmically. Never wanting to stop. I would die happily right here, with my mouth latched on to the most perfect pair of tits in the world.

Greedily, I sucked hard, taking as much of her breast into my mouth as I could, until Kira cried out sharply.

I let go with a faint pop and looked over at her.

Her pupils were dark with desire, and the air flooded with the scent of her sweet arousal.

"You okay?" I caressed her cheek, watching her carefully.

Kira hesitated for just a moment, and I caught a glimpse of that conflict within her once more. She gulped the moment that her desire won, slowly nodding.

It only took one more look into her heated gaze before my lips crashed into hers once more. My tongue caressed hers, creating slick friction. I couldn't get enough of her. Her scent was already seared into my brain. But now I couldn't pull away from the soft pressure of those hot lips. The sweet taste of her, like crisp apples and champagne.

Gods.

Kissing her was better than anything I'd ever imagined.

Kira's hands were on the front of my shirt and the moment I realized she was trying to tug the offensive material off, I sat upright and pulled my shirt off in one smooth motion, tossing it somewhere on the floor below.

Kira's face went bright red when she saw my torso—I was definitely going to use that to my advantage. Taking her hand in mine, I pressed it to my chest, helping her palm slide down the muscles of my stomach. Her hand lingered there, even when I drew mine away. Kira's breaths shuddered, and her eyes were half lidded with lust.

After wanting Kira for so long, seeing her now, so affected by my body... wanting me... it had desire churning through me at a fever pitch.

I should be taking things slow. I needed to be careful with her... but every instinct was screaming at me to press closer, to obliterate the distance between us. As I claimed Kira's lips once more and ground my hips against hers, the only thing left between us was a few flimsy layers of clothing.

I kissed her, again and again, as everything in me hummed in pure bliss, completely wrapped up in her, all while I tried and failed to talk myself into stopping. I had to stop. If I took things too far, Kira would—every thought in my head effectively died as Kira reached down and tugged off her sleeping shorts.

Oh. Fuck yes.

I dragged my pants down just far enough to free myself and slid my hardness against Kira's clit. I rubbed against her, teasing her again and again until Kira looked like she was just on the verge of coming, then stopped moving entirely.

"Tell me what you want, Baby." I murmured into her ear.

She moaned in frustration and arched her hips, seeking that bit of friction that would send her over the edge.

"I need you to say it." I said, pulling further away from her.

"Fuck me. I'm so close… please."

The sound of her begging got me harder than I'd ever been in my life. All the blood in my body went south, every thought vanished. There was nothing but Kira, laid out in front of me, wanting me.

I slid my cock down to her entrance, where her tight pussy was dripping for me. With one sharp thrust, I was deep inside her, plunging into the sweetest bliss I had ever known.

CHAPTER 6
KIRA

What the fuck was I doing? How did I go from resolving to reject Magnus forever, to begging for his fat cock?

I'll admit that I was torn when he'd first kissed me. There was some small part of me that was still clinging desperately to my last ounce of self respect. That part of me died under his warm weight on top of me, and the solid press of his muscular body against mine. He felt so good, so unbelievably good.

There was something about the way he kissed me that made all of my thoughts go fuzzy, as my fierce resolve melted like butter.

Gods. The way that Magnus touched me lit every inch of my skin on fire.

I was so fucking angry at him—and I didn't want him to stop.

I didn't want him to stop touching me, definitely not to take his hands off the sensitive peaks of my breasts.

Something about the way he touched my body like I was *his...* it made me want to scream, even as he had me on the verge of coming. Why did this man have to be so fucking fine? Minutes after he'd taunted me that he'd make me beg for it... after I'd mentally laughed in my mind that I was never going to beg for him... he'd worked my body like a finely tuned instrument, until everything in me was singing, desperate for him.

I can't believe that I actually begged for Magnus Grimson.

But when he plunged his cock into me, the delicious friction had my eyes rolling back in pure pleasure.

He was big, and I was still a little sore from last night, but I wouldn't have asked him to stop if someone was holding a knife to my neck.

Then Magnus started rocking his massive body inside of me. He pulled almost all the way out, before thrusting sharply back in. Making me feel every inch of his girth against my tender walls.

But it was his eyes. Those sharp gray eyes, hard and unyielding as steel, watching me with such hot passion that it electrified me, leaving me raw and vulnerable before him. Magnus made me feel so damn possessed, so utterly claimed—all with just one look.

Why did this feel more intense than my first time? Why was it so much different when I could see his face, the heat in his eyes locked on mine? When I knew that it was my own personal bully that was seated between my legs, slamming inside of me, over and over again?

Every time that he fucked back into me, I felt it more and more. The words that he wasn't saying. That I was *his*. That I belonged to *him*.

It was terrifying.

But the pleasure that he was building in my body made it feel like the truth. Here I was, spreading my legs wider for him, panting and moaning for him. Digging my nails into his shoulder because I needed something to ground me, because something about the way that Magnus was fucking me was ripping apart everything I thought about myself.

Then he shifted his hips in a way that had me feeling him so much deeper. It had me slipping further and further out of control.

"That's it, Baby." Magnus said, with his voice strained through with lust.

His deep voice, praising me was another caress, hitting my swollen clit with all the force of a very small bomb.

The pleasure built until I was writhing with it, powerless against it.

All of a sudden, I cried out as I came, the walls of my pussy pulsing with the force of it. White hot pleasure flooded through me, coursing down my limbs until I felt it everywhere. Felt *him* everywhere.

"Good girl." Magnus' praise made me shiver.

My legs were shaking from the force of the climax, but somehow it was his voice in my ears that had me rattled to my core.

Then Magnus sped up, slamming into me again and again like a force of nature. His thrusts were primal, almost brutal, as he sank into me, again and again, trying to lose himself in me.

I had to admit, as I watched the way he moved fluidly on top of me, that he was sort of magnificent.

"Look at you, taking me so well," he said through gritted teeth.

I have no idea why I did it, but there was something in his expression that drew me in, that had me leaning forward until I pressed a soft kiss to his lips.

Magnus groaned like I'd strangled him, like me giving him a kiss had killed him.

His steady pace stuttered, and then he slammed into me, grinding his hips against mine hard. His entire body shuddered as he came, and his cock pulsed deep inside of me.

Magnus was staring at me with a fierce look in his eyes that I just couldn't place. It was almost as if he was looking at me like he'd never seen me before.

Which didn't make any sense. None of what was happening between us was making any sense.

The moment that I caught my breath, my cheeks heated when I realized one little problem. How the hell was I going to sneak away from him? Where could I run off to? Magnus was already in my goddamn room. He was already still *inside* of me. How was I going to get away before this little entanglement got awkward?

I was sure that now he'd gotten his dick wet, that he'd taken everything that he wanted from me. Soon he'd revert back to the Magnus I knew. The one that couldn't stand the sight of me, and we'd shortly get back to fighting.

I had to get away from him before all that. I didn't think that my ego could take any more of a bruising.

I got as far as pulling my arms out from under him, in what I thought were slow and barely noticeable movements.

"Where do you think you're going?" Magnus wrapped his muscular arms around me, pulling me to his chest tighter, as if even that small distance I'd managed offended him. He kissed my cheek before whispering into the shell of my ear. "I'm not done with you yet."

CHAPTER 7
MAGNUS

Even after taking her four times, I didn't feel my desire slacken at all. I was still burning with the need to kiss her, to touch her and fill her.

I had to make her come apart under my body. Had to get my scent buried deep inside of her, so no one would forget who she belonged to, least of all *her*.

Though I had just taken her minutes ago, I felt myself hardening again, as I watched those perky round tits jiggle as Kira panted, catching her breath from everything I'd already done to her.

Kira's pussy was swollen with the prettiest red flush. I couldn't let that go to waste.

She gasped when I pressed my cock against her entrance, rubbing against her, grinding down on her clit. Kira arched her back, fisting the bed sheets as her eyes rolled back.

"Eyes on me," I stopped moving, easing the pressure off Kira's perfect little body, until she whimpered in complaint. I waited until her deep blue eyes snapped open. Looking into Kira's eyes was better than diving straight into the depths of the sea; I got lost in her.

Every time Kira gazed at me, she tensed, as if she was bracing herself for another insult or dismissal.

Fuck *me,* for doing that to her. But I was going to change it all and make things right.

I refused to give her any pleasure unless she knew exactly from whom it came. Her eyes widened as I rewarded her compliance with just the right pressure on her clit to make her lose her mind.

"Say my name," I whispered into Kira's ear, as I pressed light circles on her needy little clit.

"Say it." I dug in hard.

"Magnus!" Kira cried out helplessly.

I lined myself up against her entrance, watching as Kira licked her lips and spread her legs, making room for me.

"That's my good girl," I praised her, making Kira's cheeks burn.

I slammed into her with one hard thrust.

Kira moaned sweetly. Her eyes were half-lidded in lust, but still watching me. She didn't look away once as I began to move, thrusting into her in fast strokes.

Again and again, I showed her with my body, everything she wasn't ready to hear in words. That she was *mine.*

Kira had always been mine, and she always would be.

I thrust harder, as the thought of all the males I had fought over the years popped into my head. Males who I'd caught leering at Kira. Not that she had ever noticed. They might not have known the exact reason why I targeted them, but I never let up on a single one of them until they were more wary of me than interested in her.

Though I never allowed myself to indulge in her, it had

always been painfully obvious to me that Kira was pure perfection. More than any of the shifters in the Stonevalley pack deserved, myself included.

I didn't recognize myself, rutting into Kira, like a beast. Thrusting hard, I couldn't stop myself. I would never get enough of Kira's sweet moans, the red flush to her creamy skin that crept all the way up to her neck as she was close to coming.

"Look at how well you take me, that's it." I murmured into her ear, as I took her hand, pinning it to the bed. I jerked her hips closer to mine with my other hand, gripping her tight. Holding her in place exactly where I wanted her. Kira was completely spread out and vulnerable before me. Mine for the taking.

I thrust deeply, then ground my pelvis against the space where my body met hers, clenching her hip hard enough to bruise. Holding her tighter. Moving right over that sweet spot that would make her explode.

She was close, so close.

I could feel her walls tightening up, her breathing going wild. I could see it in the look in her eyes, how her pupils darkened as the pleasure built within her. How her eyes widened as that pure bliss began to consume her.

"So. Fucking. Gorgeous," I told her, staring straight into her eyes.

That tipped her over the edge. Kira's pussy walls pulsed all around me as she came. She cried out in a high-pitched moan, keeping her eyes locked on mine the entire time.

That's right. I was going to turn Kira from this wary little thing into my good girl in no time at all.

As soon as Kira came down from the high of her orgasm, I dropped the reins from my wolf, letting me lose the last of my control.

I snapped my hips against her fiercely, driving into her at a ruthless pace. My hold on her hips tightened as I held her exactly where I wanted her. Exactly where she needed to be. Thrusting so hard that the headboard jostled violently against the wall.

I grit my teeth as I felt the tingling in my balls, not wanting to stop, wanting to keep fucking her forever.

Until the pleasure built into a fever-pitch, overwhelming and impossible to ignore. I fucked into her deep, losing myself completely.

Pleasure like bolts of lightning shot all the way up my spine. I groaned. Grinding into her hard, my dick throbbed, unloading pulse after pulse of my cum deep inside her.

Where my scent would linger for days, maybe even weeks, scaring off every other shifter male for miles.

After what felt like forever, I finally stopped coming, and laid still on top of her, catching my breath. I would have taken her again, I'd only need a few minutes to recharge, but Kira looked exhausted.

I pulled out of her carefully, and my gaze was riveted to the sight of a trickle of cum slowly leaking out of Kira's sweet little pussy. With one finger, I scooped up every last drop that slipped on to her thigh and gently pushed it back into her.

Where it belonged.

I climbed back on top of her, kissing her deeply. Kira kissed me back in a shaky daze. Thoroughly worn out from all the rough sex.

I would ease up on her in just a minute. Get her something to eat. We had definitely missed breakfast and possibly lunch as well. We had to talk, clear up some of the mistrust that I'd built in her over the years.

But first, I had to give my cum time to settle in her.

None of my essence would drip out. It was all staying right where it needed to be, so no one would be able to question who Kira belonged to.

CHAPTER 8

KIRA

Since the Masked ball, I had let Magnus have sex with me a dozen times.

Which was insane. Last Friday, I was a virgin. I'd never even been kissed.

After I had resolved to cut him out of my life, he had somehow put me under a spell, with those steely gray eyes and the fiery passion of his hot mouth.

He was just so fucking seductive. It wasn't fair at all.

Even though we'd already done it multiple times, after we finished, I was always certain that the other shoe was going to drop. That he was going to go back to insults and degradation. That his eyes were going to turn cold and hateful. He would probably tell me that sleeping with me was nothing but a mistake.

Instead, Magnus was staring at me, with burning heat in his eyes, and a possessiveness so hot that I could feel it. His hands were in my hair, running his fingers through the strands, straightening out the curls and watching them spring back into ringlets once he let them go.

I cleared my throat. "Can you wear your gloves, later?"

Magnus paused from playing with my hair. He knew what I meant. Wearing gloves over his soulmark would be hiding our... whatever this was, from the rest of the pack.

I wasn't ready for the others to know. Not with this nagging feeling in my gut, telling me that our arrangement was held together by an illusion, and that at any moment, reality was going to come crashing through.

"If that's what you want." Magnus nodded slowly.

Perfect. We would keep things quiet. For now. Until I could make sense of what the hell was going on.

Going back to classes on Monday was *weird*.

I was sure that everyone who looked at me was going to be able to see that I had changed somehow.

After everything, all this turmoil stirring within me. After the secret kisses and making love deep within the heart of the castle... it had left a mark on me. One that I was sure that the others could see.

None of my teachers and classmates noticed a thing. Even though everything was different.

I managed to get in my seat without wincing. I guess it was a good thing that I was back to class. My body could really use a break. Even while I was soaking everything in and half certain that it was all going to end sooner rather than later, it was a lot of sex. I couldn't shake the feeling that I would have to take advantage when I still could, before our relationship went up in flames.

My first class was Advanced Astrology with Professor

Sandoval. It was the written portion of the class, so no telescopes and star charting. I opened up to my notes, and diligently copied the information from the lecture.

The lunar eclipse weakens the power of the wolf. Healing and strength wane. During the solar eclipse, wolves standing in the path of totality will—

All the hairs on my arms raised suddenly. I could feel someone's gaze on me.

Pulling the tip of my pen away from the paper, I froze, searching in my peripheral vision.

Was that Ruben?

Why was he staring at me? I think that over the years he'd said a total of three words to me.

I moved my hand across the page, writing nothing but nonsense. Watching him.

Yes, he was definitely staring at me.

Well, that was weird. He definitely hadn't stared at me before. Unless he had? Was this just the first time I was noticing it?

No. The prickle down my neck as he watched me, that was all new.

I jotted down the occasional note, trying and failing to pay attention to the impact of the eclipse on shifters. Ruben watched me the whole class period, nostrils flaring.

Was he... smelling me?

Did this mean that he could smell everything that Magnus and I had been doing?

Gods, that was so embarrassing. But what would that matter to Ruben?

I packed up everything quickly at the end of the lesson and was the first one out the door. I had to put space between me and the rest of my classmates. Walking at a brisk clip down the hall, I took off in the opposite direction of my next class.

I slumped against the castle wall, staring up at the candelabra sconces. Would it be easier to just admit to everyone that I had something going on with Magnus? And risk the embarrassment when our little dalliance ended and we parted ways? Would that be better than cutting off the embarrassment of having my shifter classmates trying to sniff out what was going on with me?

"I never took you as one of those girls." Ruben spoke a hair too fast, barely containing his excitement.

My back straightened instantly, as I noted the nearest exit in the corner of my eyes. I was so wrapped in my feeling sorry for myself that I hadn't even sensed Ruben following me.

"It makes sense. Your brother was working hard all of these years to climb rank. I wish I'd known earlier that you were looking to do the same." His eyes were narrowed, trailing up and down my body, as if he were sizing me up.

I wasn't sure what Ruben meant, so I just stared at him blankly. There was something about the way he was leering at me that put me on edge.

"I always thought that it was such a shame that you were so low rank. Such a pretty little thing like you. But if you're looking to improve your position in the pack, maybe we can come to some kind of arrangement." Ruben smiled slowly.

What did he mean by that?

Slowly he walked straight into my space. Was he trying to back me into the wall?

In one swift motion, I side-stepped him, moving into the center of the hallway.

"I'm not interested," I muttered over my shoulder.

Maybe I wasn't quite sure what his game was, but I'd had quite enough of one man in particular pushing me into corners to last me a lifetime.

Three rapid steps away down the hallway, that was as far as I got before Ruben's hand was on my shoulder, jerking me back.

"Why are you running? Because of Magnus Grimson? Do you think that spreading your legs for that hotheaded alpha is going to raise your rank?" He was gripping too hard for me to shake him off.

The wolf in me was snarling, sizing up this asshole. Ruben was in the same year as me, and he'd participated in the same coming of age ceremony, shifting to a wolf at the same time that I had. His wolf wasn't the largest, mine might be able to take him.

There would be discipline involved for going after a higher-ranked wolf, but it would mean that he wouldn't bother me again. Within me, my wolf braced herself, just waiting for the go ahead to break free. She snarled within my chest, ready to rip apart this intruder.

First, I'd try the diplomatic approach.

"Let me go."

Ruben was holding my shoulder almost directly over my soulmark, which was feeling heated and irritated. He wasn't loosening his grip at all.

"See, your problem is that you've got your sights too high. I might not be as high-ranking, but you're delusional if you think that Magnus is going to stick around for someone so below his rank." Ruben leaned in close. Puffs of carbon dioxide brushed my ear as he whispered. "I promise I'll make arrangements to keep you around. Treat me right, and I'll make sure to return the favor."

A scent that was becoming more familiar than my own

settled my wolf down, even as my human self tensed. That was all the warning I got before Ruben's hand was wrenched away from me.

I turned in time to see my soulmate, with pure rage on his face, pupils blown wide and the steely gray nothing but thin slits. *Where the hell did he come from?* Magnus slammed Ruben into the stone walls. Ruben barely had time to yelp in surprise before Magnus was on him. Biting down with wolf teeth, shredding Ruben's shoulder into a bloody mess.

"Wait, wait." Ruben's cries turned into shrieks of pain. Magnus was latched on, sharp teeth sawing deep into the muscle. His biceps tensed yanking Ruben's arm hard, until with a distinct pop, it dislocated. Magnus didn't stop until he'd ripped through both skin and muscle and Ruben's limb was torn off.

"She's not for you. She was never meant for you." Blood dripped down Magnus' sharp teeth with each word. "You keep her name out of your mouth. If I even hear you whisper her name, I will rip that tongue out as well."

Ruben's voice was high-pitched and strained as he repeated over and over, "I didn't know. I'm sorry... I'm s-sorry."

Magnus shoved Ruben's severed arm back at him, and watched with cold indifference as Ruben struggled to hold his detached arm and staunch the bleeding at the same time. "You should probably go try to see if Nurse Blanche can reattach that before it's too late."

Ruben sped down the hall without another word, stalking off like his life depended on it. In all honesty, if the chemical cocktail of adrenaline and cortisol circulating in the air around us was any indication, it did.

As soon as Ruben scurried down the hall like a rat, Magnus turned to me slowly. His gaze swept over me carefully, taking in every inch of me. His nostrils flared. Though his teeth shifted back to human, blood was still dripping down his chin.

Did he blame me for what just happened with Ruben?

I froze. Every inch of my muscles went tense.

The last couple of days fell straight out of my mind and I was left with each and every moment that he had stared me down in these dark halls. How his gaze had burned me, not with desire but something like animal hatred. All the times that he'd insulted me started to circle round and round in my head and wouldn't stop.

Get the fuck out of my way.

No one asked you to come here.

Do you think I want you anywhere near me?

Turn around. Get out of my sight if you know what's good for you.

I couldn't help it, I started shaking and couldn't stop.

Magnus reached a hand out to me and I was too terrified to move. There wasn't anything I could do. If someone like him got angry at me, that was it. He'd have me in pieces before I could even—

He tugged me close and wrapped his arms around me. He stroked soothing patterns up and down my back as he shushed me gently.

"Are you okay, Baby?" he murmured into my ear.

Tears burned in the corner of my eyes, making me feel stupid.

I was a warrior. Fighting was written into my blood, and here I was, crying like a little bitch, because some guy had been mean to me? Because I wasn't sure what was happening?

I was supposed to be better than this. But no matter what I was supposed to be, the tears fell anyway.

MAGNUS

The scent of my mate's fear stank worse than the lingering stench of that bottom feeder, Ruben Anderson.

I thought that I had doused Kira in enough of my scent that the other shifters would know better than to go anywhere near her. Apparently, I overestimated the intelligence of her classmates.

She was crying. Shaking.

Somehow, I knew that it was my fault—I never meant for my mate to feel this way. I never meant to be the source of her pain.

She tensed up as I started heading towards her.

Gods, was she scared that *I* was going to hurt *her?*

How had I let it get to this point?

I scooped up my little mate in my arms. Did I have a plan? No. But anything was better than staying here, with her panic hanging thick in the hallway, and the blood of Ruben Andersen staining the stone. I'd thought that I'd done enough to make him stay away from Kira. He wasn't one of the wolves who I'd been most worried about, sniffing around the girl I'd always secretly wanted, but he had been one of the more persistent ones.

Kira was sniffling, and clenching her eyes shut, trying to force herself to stop crying, but she wasn't tense anymore and wasn't trying to pull out of my arms. She didn't demand that I put her down, or ask her where I was taking her as I carried her through the hallways and up the stairways of the Stonevalley castle. I carried her all the way to my room.

Kira didn't even say a single word when I sat her down on a velvet ottoman. She was staring into space, as she let me undress her like a doll. I stripped Kira out of her neat little camisole and cardigan. I tugged off her trousers, expecting her to ask me what I was doing. Instead, Kira quietly let me strip her bare, without a word.

I thought about tugging off my own shirt and pants, before deciding against it. They were covered in blood anyway. What did it matter if they got ruined? With slow motions, I pulled Kira back into my arms, readjusting my hold on her as I went into my bathroom and turned on the shower. As soon as the temperature adjusted, I walked both of us under the falling water.

That snapped Kira out of wherever she had gone inside of her own head. She looked at me with wide eyes as I set her down under the spray of the shower. Carefully, I lathered up my loofah with soap, before I began to gently scrub her shoulder. Targeting the area where that asshole had touched her.

Maybe I should be saying something more to soothe her, but I wasn't going to be able to calm myself, wouldn't be able to *think straight* until the scent of another male was totally cleansed from her flesh.

Once the soap had done its work, I brought my lips to

her shoulder, kissing the skin freed from the competing male's stench. That asshole had grabbed her right on her soulmark. The thought of it made me want to hunt Ruben down all over again and finish what I had started. Why had I stopped with one arm? That whiny little rat deserved to be in the ground.

"You aren't..." Kira trailed off, looking away and biting her lip.

With one finger, I lifted her chin until she was looking straight into my eyes.

"Talk to me baby girl. Tell me what's wrong," I coaxed her. The scent of her fear had faded somewhat. She took a tentative sniff of the air surrounding us, probably checking for any hints of adrenaline and cortisol and relaxed somewhat. *That's right. That's my girl. You don't have anything to fear from me. Baby, I'm all yours.*

"I thought you were mad at me." Kira leaned in close and burrowed her head in my chest.

I wrapped my arms around her, leaning down to murmur into her ear, "It's not your fault that you're beautiful and your classmates are stupid."

Kira gasped, looking up sharply into my eyes. "You think I'm beautiful?"

What?

Kira didn't know that I thought she was attractive?

I'd been on her this whole weekend, and could barely peel myself away from her. I wanted to live for the rest of my life inside of her. Buried in her sweet depths. Even before I knew that she was my mate, she had always been the most gorgeous female I'd ever seen.

How did she not know? Well obviously, I hadn't said anything to her. But what the hell did she think we'd been doing? Had she really let me fuck her nonstop when she thought that I wasn't even attracted to her? *If only you had any idea how I live for you.*

It wasn't accurate to describe what I felt for her as an attraction. It was so much more than that. It was more like my lungs were filled with grease, and I was drowning. When she was around, I could take a breath of fresh air. It was more like my skin was on fire and she was an oasis. My insides were all twisted in a hunger only she could satisfy. I needed to devour her. I had to have her.

"I thought that I'd shown you all weekend how I feel about you." I pulled Kira closer to me, until her soft curves pressed against me. Kira was still tense, looking far away. Did she not believe me?

She didn't relax at all.

"What is it?"

"I thought that you only wanted me because of the bond," Kira said it all in a rush, like if she gave herself time to think about what she was saying, the words would get trapped inside her.

"I wanted you before the bond," I said. That much I could admit to Kira without scaring her off.

I didn't know how to do this. The only thing that my experience as a dominant wolf taught me was how to be decisive. How to protect and dominate through being the most powerful wolf. Through a mix of aggression and skill.

But this?

My mate's emotions were like a delicate web. I could sense that they were fragile... because of me. I had broken something within her. Nothing in my life had given me any experience with handling it. But I had to. I could sense that the damage I'd done still lingered.

Kira shook her head as if she didn't understand.

I didn't know what to say to fix this. I felt like anything I could say was right on the verge of making things worse. The damage I'd done already went too deep.

All I knew to do was show her what she meant to me.

If it took the rest of my life for her to heal, so be it.

I would make my atonement. As long as she was there by my side, I would spend the rest of my life making up for the pain I'd caused her.

CHAPTER 10

KIRA

T didn't understand what was happening between us at all.

I was in the shower, and Magnus was holding me.

Every inch of my body had been tense, anticipating the rage of a dominant wolf. But instead, Magnus was holding me, pressing a trail of light kisses up my neck.

He still had his clothes on. I don't know why that was the detail that was making adrenaline pound through me so hard that I could hear my own heartbeat thudding in my ears. My blood was rushing so fast that I was dizzy with it —like if Magnus wasn't holding onto me, I was on the verge of falling to the floor.

It was stupid. We'd already had sex, more than a dozen times. I don't know why the feeling of him caressing my skin *now* when he was fully clothed was making my brain fuzzy with panic.

Maybe it was because it didn't seem like he was doing this because he just wanted to fuck me.

I don't know if it was because without the distraction of

sex, the intimacy was just too raw. He was so close and holding me like he cared about me... when a part of me had whispered that this wasn't real. That he was just using me for sex and to enjoy it while I could.

He wasn't supposed to be holding me... like this. Like I mattered to him.

His soft caresses against my skin, his tender embrace was shattering all the illusions I'd built up about what this was. About what I was doing.

Now I didn't even know. I couldn't lie to myself anymore.

I wanted to break out of his hold, as much as I wanted to lean into the comforting touches.

It didn't help that my wolf was inside of me preening. She was right where she wanted to be. If I could see her right now, she would be laying on her belly with her legs splayed out all undignified, sitting in the sunlight. My wolf was completely ignoring the rising tide of anxiety within me, like she might ignore a mosquito circling my bed at night.

No help whatsoever.

What the fuck was I even doing?

Magnus must have noticed that something was off about me. He reached over me to turn off the spray of the shower. He wrapped me in towels that were fluffier than down fur, lifting me in his arms and carrying me to his bed.

The way that he was touching me right now was making the intimacy too real.

None of this was making any sense.

Did I dare to believe the words Magnus had just told me, that he had wanted me before the bond? How? What did he mean that he'd wanted me, even while insulting me and spending every moment in my presence looking angry at the fact that I'd dared to exist?

Was he trying to rewrite history? Now that he knew that I was his soulmate, was this all an act? Was he treating me now the way that he'd wished he treated me?

What would be worse? If he'd actually wanted me and treated me like shit anyway? Or if he was talking himself into believing that he'd always wanted me—like he was a powerful enough shifter that he'd be able to rewrite time.

Now Magnus was pulling his shirt off over his head. I never would have believed it if someone had told younger me that watching Magnus Grimson take off his shirt would be what calmed down my anxiety.

This is what I understood—the raw, primal need. The uncontrollable and wild desire brewing between us.

His pants followed soon after. His belt buckle clicked, and then the fabric pooled around his legs, freeing all of him.

A shiver of anticipation slid down my spine as I waited for him to initiate *more*. My skin heated with the memory of his touch, the soft caresses that lit a fire in me... but all Magnus did was wrap his arms around me over the towel and pull me close. His nose brushed against the shell of my ear as he breathed me in deeply. He was holding me like I was delicate and precious. Like I was made of glass. Like he wanted me for something more than a quick and dirty fuck. More than scratching that wild itch within him.

As he held me, the heated warmth of anticipation was replaced by fear in an instant, like I had fallen through the ice, plunging in over my head.

I didn't know what was happening between us at all.

CHAPTER II
MAGNUS

Every moment that I wasn't buried inside of Kira, I could feel her slipping away from me.

I couldn't wrap my head around it. She let me fuck her—was eager for it. It was clear in her scent that she wanted me just as much as I wanted her. But as soon as we were done, Kira acted like a hunted animal, withdrawing into herself. She would wander into her own head with a faraway expression on her face. The air would stink with the sharp acid of her anxiety. Kira never went so far as to pull away from me, but I could feel the tension in her muscles when I tried to hold her after taking her.

It was driving me crazy.

I felt like I was losing her before I ever got a chance to have her.

It drove me to find her throughout the castle, over and over again. In-between her classes, before meals, whenever I could find her on her own. I'd stalk her down. Push her into empty rooms throughout the castle and fuck her until she saw stars.

At least when I was rutting deep inside of Kira's tight

walls, I could make her scream my name. I could stare into her eyes as she came around my cock, forcing her to acknowledge just where she was getting her pleasure.

For a short while at least, I could make her as desperate for me as I was for her.

While I had her under me, writhing in pleasure, maybe I'd be able to fuck her hard enough to break through the walls that she'd built between the two of us.

Maybe if I did it enough, the message would finally sink through, that the two of us belonged together.

I'd go to her over and over, driving myself deep inside of her until she could feel the truth in her bones. Kira was mine.

If I had to fuck the truth into her, so be it. For as long as it took, I'd make her see it, too.

MY WOLF WAS GETTING AGITATED. I could feel him prowling beneath my ribcage, scratching at my bones. I was reaching the limit that my beast could tolerate staying away from Kira. I wouldn't be able to focus on any of these reports. I wouldn't be able to fucking think when the wolf within me was so close to the surface, and sharpening his claws on my organs.

If I didn't seek her out, he would simply burst through my skin and find her.

The stink of Kira's fear, the tense way that she was holding herself around us—it was driving my wolf mad.

I snapped the notebook on my desk shut, abandoning my work.

I was falling behind on my duties. Not enough that anyone would give me shit about it, but enough that they would start to notice.

It wasn't like I had any choice. Even if I wanted to fight my wolf, there was no denying the pull that I felt to her. I was about at the end of my tether as well.

I had to find her. To reassure myself that Kira was alright.

It should have been enough that my scent was all over her. Kira wasn't ready for the two of us to go public with our relationship, so I had to resort to more primitive ways to mark her as mine. I'd flooded her with so much of my cum, one would have to be a fool to miss the hidden message that she was not to be touched.

But that idiot, Ruben Anderson, still thought that he had a right to put his hands on her. How many more Rubens were lurking around *my* woman, waiting for a chance at her?

I strode quickly through the halls of the castle... plagued by nonstop thoughts of Ruben or some other idiot panting after her, putting their filthy hands on her. Ornate sconces blurred as my pace quickened. Through the cold stone hallways and hidden passageways, I ran to my mate.

Even if I didn't have her scent burned deep in my brain, and her schedule memorized, I could have followed the tug of the bond to her. I could feel it within me like a physical presence, as if there was a cord stretched thin, always reaching out to its other half.

Now that the bond was awakened between the two of us, I wondered how it was ever possible that I didn't know it was her. The bond was alive, burning and itching deep in my bones when we were left apart for too long. I could follow this tug in my chest to her as easily as I could follow the trail of any prey animal in the forest.

Kira's presence through our soul connection was like an echo of my own heart-beat. It felt as if I could just rip out the thin barrier between us and be able to swim in her skin. Kira was more than the woman I'd lusted after in secret for my entire life. *She was the other half of my soul.*

Kira's discomfort and tension around me was worse than any physical pain I'd ever experienced. It was a thorn straight to the heart—if she ever truly pulled away from me, I would bleed out.

I had to give her time. I *knew* that I had to give her time.

I had to remind myself that our connection was new. Kira needed to adjust to our relationship, and I needed to give her space.

I could be patient. I would wait as long as she needed. As long as she was mine and everyone knew it.

It didn't take long before I found her. She was in-between classes, if my memory was correct, she was just leaving her Lupine History class. Kira walked alone, holding her textbooks in a tight grip in front of her chest.

I hid in the dark of the hallway, watching her walk steadily closer to me. As soon as she passed, I grasped her by the crook of the elbow, yanking her against my chest.

Kira gasped in surprise, but the scent of her shock quickly shifted into arousal when she recognized me. She leaned into me, letting her head roll back. Exposing her neck to me, and all that sweet skin... as if she trusted me.

I pressed my palm against her belly, holding her tight to me. I wanted to wrap myself around her as if I was a second skin. I leaned down until my nose was right in the crook of her neck, wanting to breathe her in.

For a moment, I just held her, basking in the feeling of

rightness. I wasn't yearning for the missing pieces; my other half was right here.

But it didn't take long before my touches turned hungry. I slipped my hand under her blouse, seeking more of her silky skin. Needing more of her.

I traced a path across the impossibly soft skin of her stomach, until I was brushing against her sweet curves. I cupped her breast, feeling the weight of it as I slid my finger against her nipple, teasing her until it hardened into a tight point.

Kira whimpered as I fondled her, leaning against me, and the sound of her little cry of pleasure drove me wild. I was already rock hard for her and straining against my trousers. Grinding against her ass for relief, I was half-mad with the need to feel her around me. I growled, struggling to contain myself. Fighting and losing the war to hold myself back. To let the moment last and just luxuriate in her presence.

I ached with the need to bury myself in her. My cock strained against the fabric that kept me from her. Yearning for her hot cunt. Needing to be swallowed up by her tight walls.

As I ground my hardness against her, Kira let out a throaty moan—instantly shredding the last of my patience.

She was wearing a long skirt, and I jerked the fabric up, getting it out of my way. Her sweet pussy was right there, the shape of it fully visible under thin cotton. I jerked the offending fabric out of the way, needing her too badly to pull it down. Not now, when the smell of her arousal was all around me. Now when she was in my arms and I could feel the warmth of her, so close.

I needed her now.

Fabric tore as I unzipped my trousers, in my haste to get to her.

Nothing existed but the throbbing ache in my cock, the tingling in my balls and the glistening wetness of Kira's perfect little pussy.

Then I was sinking into the silky velvet of her heat. Straight into the greatest bliss I'd ever known.

CHAPTER 12
KIRA

There was nothing easier in the world than to give in as my mate seduced me. His hands on my skin were like slipping into a hot bath. Like floating into bubbly bliss.

He was all around me, his scent as familiar as a tattoo on my brain. All his firm muscles were a wall at my back.

So strong... he'll keep me safe.

I needed every ounce of his strength... I was fragile enough to shatter into pieces and he was the only thing grounding me, holding me together.

Once again, Magnus had found me in-between my classes. Like the times before, it never took long at all for me to give in to the pleasure. I leaned into his caress, seeking out more of his touch as his hands roamed familiar paths across my body. The way that he touched me lit my skin on fire. I never felt more alive than I did right now, panting and moaning as he pressed hot kisses to every inch of my skin he could reach.

I'd never felt more helpless... drowning in pleasure,

surrendering to the never-ending onslaught of bliss that only he could awaken in me.

Magnus made me so wet; I was dripping for him.

It didn't take long for his touches to change. For his hands on me to become hungrier. His grip was harder, pinching in at places. I welcomed his roughness. How his strong hands ripped the clothing between us in his desperation to have me.

Then suddenly he was prodding me, right where I needed him.

There was nothing better than the abrupt fullness as he thrust sharply into me. Nothing hotter than the harsh stretch, as his thick girth pierced through my emptiness. Nothing sweeter than the delicious friction as he started to move. Pounding. Holding my hips in a punishing grip, right where he wanted me.

He fucked me hard.

Magnus was too on edge, too close to his wolf to make this gentle—which was perfect. I *craved* his aggression. Welcomed him in as he slammed into me so deep that I could feel him in my stomach. So deep that I could barely tell anymore where he stopped and I began.

He held on to my hips in a bruising grip, keeping me in place at just the right angle so that each sharp upward thrust hit a spot inside of me that made me lose control.

All I could feel was his big cock moving within me, sliding against my walls with a friction so delicious, it was making me lose my mind. Building pressure deep in my lower belly with a slow burning tension, slowly tying every thread of me into knots. My whole world narrowed down to this—his thickness, the heat of him, how the relentless pounding somehow made me feel safe... how this felt as natural as the beating of my own heart.

Suddenly, the tension shattered into white hot bliss. I moaned, high-pitched and desperate, and reached out for my mate, just needing to hold on to him as every part of me broke apart into pleasure.

My eyes rolled back, my legs were shaking, and if he hadn't been holding on to me so firmly, I would have fallen straight to the ground. I leaned back, resting my head against Magnus as I caught my breath, utterly spent.

Magnus groaned as he quickened his pace. As he started to pound into me faster. His careful rhythm lost as he rutted into me mindlessly. His thrusts stuttered, before he dove into me hard, grinding against my hips as deep as he could go.

Then I was filled with the warmth of his spend, as his cock pulsed within me in thick spurts.

My wolf was preening within me, satisfied by the feeling of her mate's essence flooding me. She was licking her chops, and settling down, rolling onto her back, belly up and ready for a snooze.

My animal lust was sated, settling down like a predator laying down to digest her kill. But once the haze of desire cleared from my mind, it was like I was dunked into ice water.

Without the desire for him clouding my every thought, I could remember what had come before… the things he'd said to me… things that even now cast their shadow across all of our stolen moments together.

My past was a never-ending darkness in my mind. Nothing I did could shake it.

Without being able to control it, my thoughts flashed to the memory of walking down the hallways and hearing snarls. Wild and dangerous, and so menacing that even the distance of years did nothing to stop the chill that went down my spine... how all the hairs raised on my arms.

How could I overcome the trigger for my worst fears, when he was right behind me, holding me?

I can remember the exact look in Magnus' eyes. The pure hatred there... no matter what I tried, it wasn't something that I could just get over. I couldn't forget it. Couldn't forget how contempt dripped from each syllable. Nothing would erase from my mind the words he'd snarled at me. *Get the fuck out of here.*

I'd never forget how he'd said it like he had wanted to hurt me.

What the hell was I doing?

He was still inside of me, holding my hips firmly, pressing his cock in me deep. He was still throbbing and twitching... still pumping me full of his cum.

After sex, his touches always turned gentle. Brushing his hands along my body in soft caresses. Like suddenly, I was made of glass. He pressed featherlight kisses against my shoulder and neck. Wrapping his arms around me like he couldn't get enough of me.

But even so, I couldn't see him as a lover.

CHAPTER 13

KIRA

R uben never returned to his classes.

The hospital matron managed to coax his arm back on to the rest of his body.

Which honestly didn't surprise me. The Matron was an older shifter. She'd treated people through decades of the wolf wars between the Stonevalley and Edgeriver packs.

No one was talking about the fact that Ruben had dropped out of all our shared classes. I didn't so much as smell him in the same corridors as I used to. It was so weird, after having classes in the same cohort as him for years... that now he was just gone.

It was because of Magnus.

No... that wasn't quite true. It was because of me.

It made sense that Ruben thought that I was whoring myself out... What else was he supposed to think when I was drenched in the scent of a man who I didn't acknowledge as my mate? No wonder Ruben thought I was just easy. This was all because I couldn't just make it clear to the rest of the pack that I'd found my soulmate and instead hid my mark under my clothes like a coward.

How could I tell everyone I was bonded to Magnus when I had no idea what I even wanted?

Part of me rebelled against announcing to the rest of the pack that Magnus was my mate.

But we couldn't just dance around each other forever...

We couldn't hold each other in the safety of the dark and pretend that we had nothing to do with each other in the light of day. No self-respecting wolf would deal with that kind of relationship forever. Especially not a high-ranking wolf like Magnus. Eventually, he would have to move on to a partner more fitting for his station. There were plenty of she-wolves who would love to be seen on his arm.

I tried and failed to ignore the rebellion in the pit of my stomach at the thought of Magnus moving on from me and choosing another wolf to call his own. Possessive anger flooded through me as a tiny voice in my head whispered *mine.*

How could I be with him?

How could I let him go?

THE DINING HALL was filled with a heady mix of rich scents. Beef tallow. Garlic and rosemary. Thyme, black pepper and cloves. There was savory venison and a tart burst of berry. Delicious. The scents were almost intoxicating enough to get me excited to sit through the entirety of this formal dining affair.

Sleek and silky white tablecloths covered the long

tables that marked the seating ranks. The foremost table was reserved for the Alpha's heir and his family. The next tables held the high ranked betas, war generals, top soldiers and... Magnus Grimson.

About as far as one could get from him, I sat next to my brother at the table for the lowest ranking of the gammas—wolves who were more likely to be responsible for washing the tablecloths and who barely had a right to be here amongst the fighters at all.

I was wearing one of my three good dresses, the light blue cotton, with long embroidered sleeves. Dining etiquette was formal, even for the low-ranking wolves seated far in the back.

"Why aren't you sitting with him?" Sylas grumbled, glaring at his empty plate. For my brother the worst part of losing rank wasn't the change in social status so much as the change in his dinner experience. Our gamma table was always served last—at least that was the only inconvenience that my brother let me hear about.

Technically, Sylas had already worked his way through the ranks for long enough that he could move to one of the lower beta tables. He would already be eating if he moved.

I knew why he had never made the switch. Sylas refused to leave me all alone.

He would never abandon me here.

I didn't give myself away by looking across the dining hall to where Magnus sat, I didn't have to. I could feel my soulmate's attention on me. I could feel the force of all that rippling dominant wolf power.

I just shook my head.

I didn't want to go over it. There were too many curious ears, and especially those with a heightened sense of lupine hearing around. I didn't want them to find out. Next, everyone in the pack would all form an opinion about Magnus' new soulmate before I even had the chance to understand what I wanted and where this was going.

Sylas' eyes went hard, and he leaned down to whisper, "He didn't want to acknowledge you?"

"Other way around." I admitted.

Magnus would jump at the chance to let everyone know I was his mate. If I approached him right now and revealed my soulbond mark to the rest of the pack, he would be ecstatic.

I couldn't understand why he was so eager for me, when he'd also been the one who was so quick to tear me down before.

I didn't understand my soulmate at all.

Sylas leveled a cold look at me, demanding an explanation.

I sighed.

"I just need time. I need to figure out what I want." Even as I tried to explain, I could tell that my words sounded weak, even to me.

I'd already had weeks. More than that, in fact... the Masked Ball was around three months ago, and nothing had gotten resolved between Magnus and I.

I didn't know what to say about the jolt of pure anxiety I got around Magnus whenever my wolf was at rest.

It didn't make sense, because obviously I wanted Magnus too.

Even if I managed to explain to Sylas how twisted up I felt about my soulmate, would he understand me? Would he just tell me to get over it?

"What are you waiting for?" Sylas kept his face carefully blank. He was doing his best to hide his emotions, but he couldn't hide the way he'd tightened his jaw. Nor the bitter scent of frustration wafting from him, before it disappeared into the varied mix of scents in the hall.

It was always worse talking to my brother before dinner. Hunger made him quick to anger. That, and the indignity of being served last, when he had the blood of shifter generals flowing through his veins.

I just didn't get Sylas' relentless pursuit of climbing rank. It seemed like Sylas would sacrifice anything in order to elevate the two of us to what he thought was our rightful place in the pack. But I'd never be able to understand. Not when Sylas had done everything in his power to shield me from all the shit we'd been exposed to after we'd lost our status in the first place.

Honestly, if Magnus hadn't been there to beat my brother at every opportunity, Sylas would have had a far easier time rising through the ranks. It was just near impossible for anyone else to shine from under Magnus' shadow.

If I was acknowledged as Magnus' mate, Sylas and I would both be welcomed with the rest of the high betas. We would finally regain everything we'd lost when our parents died. I could see why Sylas was frustrated. The moment that Magnus was actually useful to his goals, I was refusing to cooperate.

But how to make my brother understand?

"I'm afraid of him," I admitted in a whisper.

"What the fuck did he do?" Sylas glared across the room at my mate with murder in his eyes.

This conversation was getting all fucked up. Now if I wasn't careful, Sylas was going to launch himself at my mate and start a full-fledged battle for my honor, right in the middle of dinner.

"No, it's not like that. He didn't do anything," I whispered back in a rush, before the night ended with an eruption of teeth and claws and someone in the hospital wing.

"Then why?" Sylas' nostrils flared as he demanded the truth.

A truth I didn't even understand myself.

"I... I can't get it out of my head. How he used to yell at me to get out of his way." As soon as I got the words out, I felt shaky. I felt small.

I felt exactly how I did in that hallway, when Magnus had glared at me like he'd hated me. Like I was worse than filth.

Everyone in the pack ignored me, like I wasn't even a wolf at all, but some sort of parasite. Like I was the worst thing that could happen to a shifter wolf.

But no one said anything to my face. No one but Magnus.

"But that was before he knew that you were his soulmate," Sylas said the words slowly, as if he was kindly trying to explain a very simple concept to an idiot. "Is he not acting like a proper mate now?"

I swallowed, feeling like I was pushing down an important part of myself. Feeling like I was being rushed into accepting a match that would make things convenient for everyone.

A match that would make everyone happy—everyone but me.

"He treats me fine now." I took a deep breath, to push back the panic rising to the surface. This was Sylas—he cared about me... so why did I feel like I was getting backed into a corner? "But that doesn't erase the hurt he caused before. I'm just really confused... I know that I want him, but being with him feels terrifying. Like I know he'd never hurt me, but I'm just waiting to get hurt again. Does that make sense to you?"

"Honestly, no." Sylas shook his head slowly. "Your emotions are giving me whiplash."

I couldn't look at him. I closed my eyes, trying to drown everything out. Wishing that I was anywhere but here.

If my brother... the one person who understood me better than anyone... the person who'd stood by my side after *everything* and practically raised me... if he couldn't understand what I was feeling, who could?

Maybe I just wasn't making any sense.

"What do you think I should do?" I looked down at my empty plate. I couldn't look at him.

"Talk to him. Give him a chance to explain." Sylas cast a disdainful look around the table at the older crowd of gamma wolves surrounding us. "Accepting him would be the best thing for you."

"You're right. I'll try," my voice wavered, like I was nothing but a child.

It should have worried me that I wasn't even sad. More than anything else, all the uncertainty around my soulmate relationship was just making me feel numb.

I was so tired of my fears. So tired of fighting my desire for my soulmate.

So tired of being told that everything I was feeling was wrong.

It didn't matter what choice I made. In the pack's eyes, I would be fucking up the best thing that had ever happened to me. Either that, or I'd choose something that was wrong for me.

There was no winning.

CHAPTER 14

KIRA

I waited until Magnus started to soften inside of me. Waited until his touches slowed from hungry to sleepy satisfaction and his heavy pants settled as he caught his breath.

Magnus had grabbed me on the way back from my Advanced Astrology class. The moment I separated from my classmates and was in the corridor alone, he was on me. Magnus pushed me into an empty classroom, straight on top of a dusty desk, and had taken me roughly. Fast and dirty, he'd pounded me onto the desk so hard we were in danger of tipping over and cracking the wood.

Now he was pressing his forehead against mine, staring into my eyes with a look that was adoring, and holding me like he never wanted to let me go.

A part of me wanted to wrap my arms around him and give in. It would be so easy to let him have me and hope for the best.

Another not insignificant part of me was jittery and panicked and looking for a chance to make my escape from him. To leave and get somewhere safe.

I couldn't leave things like this. I had to do something about it.

"Magnus?"

He looked up sharply. I said his name so rarely when I wasn't screaming it in pleasure.

All the attention of a large and very powerful shifter male was focused on me. I wanted to find the part of me that was quivering like a little mouse and shake some sense into her. This was my mate.

"We need to talk." I swallowed.

Magnus nodded.

He pulled himself out of me, slowly, without once looking away from the pussy he'd just thoroughly fucked. I felt the brush of his index finger against my thigh as he gathered up all the cum that had slipped out of me, pushing it back inside.

He always did that.

Then, carefully, he pulled my underwear back on and smoothed my skirt back down from where he'd bunched it up around my waist, brushing away all the wrinkles in the fabric. When he finished sorting out my outfit, Magnus took my hand, muttering, "come on."

I let Magnus hold my hand. Might as well—we were already fucking. It would probably be weird to reject hand-holding when I was letting him stick his penis in me.

Magnus led me through the castle, taking the least used and dustiest hallways that hadn't seen a deep clean since years before I was born. Through grimy, spider web encrusted pathways, and dark staircases all the way back to a small unassuming door. It opened to the pristine wing of the castle that housed the generals—filled with plush carpets, gilded portraits, and golden chandeliers. He held my hand firmly, all the way into his room.

I sat down on Magnus' bed… a bed that he had fucked me on dozens of times, but had never invited me to sleep on.

To be fair, I was always antsy after sex. Magnus was most likely respecting my boundaries by not pressing for more. Between the two of us, I was the one holding things back from progressing into a real relationship—from whatever *this* was.

Magnus sat beside me, refusing to let go of my hand. He was gazing intently into my eyes, waiting for me to say whatever it was that I had to say.

I opened my lips, and the words died on my tongue.

How was I going to say it? What was I even going to say?

Accepting him would be the best thing for you…

Sylas was right.

Isolation and rejection are hard on a pack animal…

The rest of the pack was right. This was the soulbond— it went beyond anything that my human mind could possibly comprehend.

My wolf had already accepted him… he was the other half of me. The one that the goddess had chosen for me. I *had* to accept him.

It was what everyone wanted. What my *own body* wanted.

So why did it feel like the walls were closing in on me? Why did it feel like saying the words were pounding the nails into my own coffin?

It didn't matter. I had to say it. I had to make it right. Even if those little words… that were just out of reach… even if they were killing me inside… I *had* to.

Magnus lifted my chin with one finger, forcing me to look into his eyes.

"You want me, but you're afraid of me." Magnus brushed his fingers against my cheek as he put into words everything I hadn't been confident enough to say. "I can smell the fear on you. It's driving me mad."

His nostrils flared, taking in the bitter scent of the fear that no matter what I did, wouldn't go away. Magnus sighed deeply.

My shoulders drooped as I hunched in on myself.

It wasn't supposed to be like this.

When I was little, I'd pictured being with my soulmate—every shifter did. There were enough happy couples around the Stonevalley pack to make it clear that it wasn't just some smoke and mirrors bit of magic. The soulmates I saw were *happy*. Seeing them together just made sense.

My own parents were soulmates in love—too much in love. My father lost the will to live and passed on a few weeks after Mom died.

I guess Sylas and I weren't enough for him to keep living for.

I never assumed that I would find my soulmate easily. Some shifter wolves waited for decades for their other halves to appear. But I also never pictured that when I finally found my other half, that there would be so much tension between us.

How could the two of us ever be happy? I just couldn't see how it was even possible.

Maybe a happily ever after was for other people... Maybe there was just something wrong with me. Some-thing broken deep within me... something that made me impossible to love.

Magnus pushed me down onto his bed. He grabbed my wrists, holding them above my head. He settled his weight over me, using his knee to push between my legs. It was so easy for him to hold me down and pin me in place until there wasn't anywhere for me to go.

"What would it take for you to stop being afraid?" Magnus whispered into my ear. I could feel him growing hard against my thigh as the room steadily flooded with the scent of his arousal.

Suddenly, he ground himself right in between my legs, pressing his dick against my tender pussy. "What would it take for you to want more than just this?" Magnus whispered, his lips lingering by the shell of my ear.

He had me panting. Shaking.

I wanted to spread my legs wider and just take him again. I wanted to tell him that I'd do anything he wanted. I'd be his good girl—whatever he wanted me to be. So long as he gave me another hit of that pleasure only he could give me.

I had to force myself to stop.

No.

What was Magnus *doing*?

He couldn't just seduce me into having a relationship with him.

"What if I don't want anything more than this?" I bit my lip, holding back a moan as Magnus ground against me... teasing me with all the sweet friction guaranteed to make me lose my mind.

"You don't want more?" Magnus' voice was dark and seductive, as he used his free hand to push the fabric between us out of the way, jerking my underwear to the side so that he could feel the growing wetness between my thighs. His fingers slid to my aching clit, pressing in a circular motion that made my breath hitch. "I could protect you... give back all the status, all the power that was ripped away when you were young. Make the wolves of this pack bow down in respect for you. I'd make you my fucking *queen*."

My breaths were ragged... What was he doing to me? Was it the sweet promise in his words, as he offered me the world? Or the unerring pressure he was putting on my clit? All I knew was that he was giving me the perfect friction to just forget everything—all of our differences and just *feel*.

"Anything and everything you want, I can give it to you." Magnus' eyes were hooded with desire, all of his attention locked on me.

I believed him.

He meant every single word.

Magnus was ready to give me all the pleasure and power that I could ever hope for... and the only thing that was stopping him was me.

"Even if I wanted to take your offer... what would you want in return?"

"Just you." Magnus pressed his hardness against me, letting me feel his desire. "I want everyone to see you by my side. For everyone to know that you belong to me."

Magnus was offering me... *everything*. He was making it easy for me, handing everything I could possibly want on a silver platter.

It was the entire reason I came here, to have this conversation. Everything that I had lost... that my brother had fought so hard for us to get back... for *years*. Now it was within reach.

All I had to do was say yes.

Magnus was steadily increasing the pressure on my clit, creating the perfect storm—the friction, the heat of his touch, the way that he knew exactly what I liked. How he was ready and willing to give it to me—give it *all* to me.

His big hand on my clit was right where I needed it and

his voice was a deep rumble that I could feel reverberating from in his chest... it all churned inside of me. Coiling the tension in my lower belly, tighter and tighter—until I shattered into white hot bliss.

I moaned, drowning in pleasure, powerless to do anything but let the waves of my climax pull me under. As the pleasure was still thrumming through me, pulsing from deep in my core, down my spine, and to every square inch of my body, Magnus leaned close to whisper, "You don't need to be afraid of me, Baby." He let go of my wrists, and began working on the belt of my skirt, loosening it. Slowly, he dragged both my skirt and underwear down my legs, baring me completely. "Let me show you what it would mean to be with me without fear."

He shucked off his pants, freeing his cock. His erection was so hard that it sprung straight up, slapping against the muscles of his abs.

As I watched him, eyes hooded with lust, still half lost to the force of the orgasm he'd just wrung out of me, Magnus positioned himself in between my spread legs. With one smooth thrust, he slid inside of me.

Goddess, damn.

I loved that part—how I stretched around him... How completely he filled me... Magnus felt so impossibly good. I moaned, helplessly. No matter how many times we'd fucked, I was taken aback every time by how *good* it felt.

His lips met mine in a burning kiss. Magnus took my mouth roughly. His lips moved against mine with something akin to desperation, letting me taste the depths of his hunger. Deepening the kiss, Magnus plundered into my mouth, caressing my tongue with slick pressure and sweet friction.

He tasted as good as sin. Like everything I'd ever wanted.

Then he began to move, rocking into me slowly, like we were coming together in a primitive dance. Soon, the sinuous movements of his hips against mine had me moaning all over again. Tentatively, I began to rock my hips, meeting his. Chasing after the low burn of pleasure that Magnus had lit within me.

This wasn't anything like the quick, rough fuck in an abandoned classroom. This felt like I meant more to him than some warm body that he could use to get off...

This felt like he was making love to me...

It should have terrified me. It would have terrified me if I hadn't been lost to the perfect synchronization of our hips moving together.

Right now, nothing existed but *him*—how perfect the weight of his body felt on top of me. Inside me. Nothing existed but the need to rock against him, to chase after the pleasure he was building steadily with each delicious thrust.

Nothing in my life had ever felt more perfect, more *right*, than I felt in this moment. Here and now, panting under my soulmate, his eyes on mine with a look that was dark and utterly possessive.

I could almost forget that it was Magnus Grimson who was making me feel this way.

The way that the two of us came together in bed... it was as natural as breathing.

Maybe it had been a mistake to fight against this. It was more than fighting against destiny—I was fighting against myself. It was like I was running from what I actually wanted.

Why the hell was I running from something that felt so *good?*

This was mine... this very strong and dominant alpha. He could be all mine.

I just had to say yes.

The heat of his eyes on mine was searing as Magnus rhythmically thrust into me. He didn't even look quite the same as he did when he used to bully me... not now, with his expression filled with nothing but burning devotion.

I reached out and caressed his cheek, feeling the rough stubble and the warmth of his skin.

"Fuck," Magnus cursed, clenching his eyes shut.

His even pace stuttered, and he slammed into me deep, groaning. Pulses of warmth flooded into my lower belly.

Did he just come? All because I touched his cheek once?

Panting, catching his breath, Magnus held me against him tightly, like he never wanted to let me go.

Then Magnus whispered, so softly that it sounded like words uttered in a dream.

"I love you."

CHAPTER 15

KIRA

I love you.

That couldn't be real. There was no way that those words were something that Magnus really meant.

He pulled out of me gently, pressing a soft kiss to my temple before collapsing onto the bed and promptly falling asleep. He still had one burly arm wrapped possessively around my waist as he began to snore lightly.

But what if it was real?

What did it mean to be loved by a shifter like Magnus Grimson?

Magnus was never going to let me go. He was holding on to me too tightly, and I would *never* be able to make him loosen his grip.

No. Not a wolf like him. He was too strong. Too possessive.

My lungs were too tight—I couldn't breathe.

The air was constricting all around me. I had to get out.

I just needed to get out of this room. The air was thick

with his scent and it was suffocating. I needed a moment just to breathe.

I couldn't be here. I had to break out and *go*. Now. Before it was too late.

It was already too late. It was too late the moment that I bumped into him in that masked ballroom. The moment that his mark was burned into his skin. Maybe it was something already written by fate, written into our destinies. The two of us were inevitable.

If the stories were true, we were born with one soul that was cruelly ripped apart into two. What choice did I have? How would I ever be able to escape from his grasp when the two of us shared one soul?

Slowly, slowly, I moved out from under Magnus' arm. I inched away from him, in motions that were painfully small. The entire time, I swallowed nervously as I fought to move smoothly. Couldn't make any sharp movements, couldn't jostle him.

Goddess, *please*, just let him stay asleep.

My heart was pounding the entire time that I slipped out from under his arm... I'd been so certain that I'd made a wrong move, and his dark gray eyes would snap open and lock on me.

But no. As I gently pulled away from him, Magnus still slept, unaware.

I sat up on the bed, creeping to the edge without making a single creak, and then I was away from him. I crept over to my discarded skirt and underwear that were hastily tossed to the floor. Watching Magnus nervously for any signs that he was starting to stir, I dressed. Ready to bolt if he so much as twitched. Cursing to myself at the slight clink of my skirt—why did I have to pick my only skirt with a belt?

I panicked... all while Magnus snored on.

I stepped out of his room, closing the door softly behind me without a backward glance. Moving swiftly, I retraced the dusty forgotten passages all the way through the castle, not stopping until I made it all the way to the forgotten exit by the stables.

I had no plan, no idea what I was even doing. All I could do was keep walking, each step taking me further from the castle and everyone I'd ever known. My family, my teachers, my pack... my mate. They were all behind me, out of sight. None of them were here to give me their half-hearted praise. To tell me I was doing all the *right things*.

As soon as I reached the tree line, I wasn't thinking.

I ran.

CHAPTER 16

MAGNUS

I woke up to a bed that was cold and empty—that was nothing new. I'd always woken up alone, every day of my life.

But this was different.

It wasn't that I had expected Kira to see things differently after our last conversation. I hadn't expected her to stay, not even after I'd admitted to her how deeply I'd always felt about her.

Why would she? I'd fallen asleep without even inviting her to stay.

No. This wasn't about Kira not being here.

There was something off in the air.

I drew on my wolf senses, sniffing sharply... concentrating, and I found it. Kira's lingering scent in the room was filled with the bitter tang of fear, in sharp spikes of cortisol and adrenaline.

Why would she leave me in a panic?

My wolf howled in my chest, scratching at my bones, demanding to be let out, and I didn't question his desperate need to get to her. Didn't stop to even shuck off my clothes before my wolf erupted out of me, ripping through fabric and tearing out of my body to break free. He barely stopped as my bones snapped, rearranging their shape, as my jaw stretched forward, tearing through my skin.

I barely managed to rip my bedroom door open before my thumb snapped away from my palm and shifted up to the back of what was now my wolf's paw.

My vision shifted to muted yellows and blues as all the scents crystallized in the air. My four paws hit the ground, and I bolted—following the trail Kira left as she stumbled out of my room in a blind panic. From the concentration of her scent in the air, she had left a little over an hour ago.

My wolf was running on pure adrenaline as he barreled down the Stonevalley castle hallways. Desperation burned in the pit of his stomach—a desperation that I knew not to question. His instincts were fueled by blood and claws and the need to survive, and now those same instincts were screaming at my wolf that something was wrong with my mate.

I didn't have to fully understand to know not to question my wolf's panic.

Some of the human members of the Stonevalley pack, launched out of the wolf's way. There were some startled screams and confused howls from other wolves in the pack as they saw me—one of the youngest shifter generals—running through the hallways. Tension ran high. I knew exactly what they were wondering. Were we being summoned off to another war? Was there danger within the castle?

I ignored them all.

Through the hallways, I sprinted across the castle, following her scent through the stables. The horses shrieked in alarm, I could hear them squeal and kick at the stalls behind me as I passed the aisle, not stopping until I slammed the exit door open, following Kira's trail.

Her scent was distinctly human as she headed straight into the heart of the forest.

What the hell was she doing?

Why hadn't she even bothered to shift? What was she planning? Her path led away from the Stonevalley territory. Away from any of the packs, in a patch of unclaimed land in between the shifters.

Where was she even going? There was nothing out there.

I would have understood the desire to go and shift into her wolf. Sometimes I also felt the call of the wolf within me, especially close to the full moon—I understood the need to *run*.

But she was running through the woods as a human.

The sky was darkening, and there were dangerous creatures about in the older, denser parts of the forest. Even though her shifter scent would be enough to give some creatures pause, she was vulnerable out there. No matter how fierce my little fighter could be, she was just one wolf separated from the pack.

Sharp piercing pain, split open my shoulder.

My wolf snarled in rage, putting together the pieces before I could even grasp what was going on. He ignored the pain, digging his claws deep into the earth—he stormed down her trail, his paws hurtling across the land faster than I'd ever moved before.

Through my wolf's reaction, I understood.

The pain that I'd felt, it didn't have anything to do with me. There should have been the iron tang of my own blood, but instead nothing. Just the echoes of pain branding into my neck.

I wasn't sliced open by some stray branch, or some rabid animal with a death wish.

No.

My wolf dug his claws deep into the earth. Panic driving him forward.

Kira.

Something—somewhere—had hurt my mate.

As I felt the pain, burning deep into my shoulder, corrosive as acid and bone-deep, I sent out a silent prayer to the universe, to the gods, to whoever could hear me. To whoever would listen...

Please, let me get to her before it was too late.

CHAPTER 17

KIRA

I panted sharply. The cold air felt like shards of glass piercing me from the inside.

My heels sunk into the soft earth as I ran. My legs were burning, and my feet were numb. The curly strands of my hair whipped behind me in the wind.

It felt amazing.

There was a stitch on my side, and my muscles were protesting. I'd been running for miles already, dodging tree roots and vegetation in impractical footwear.

I'd planned about as far as each next step I took... steps that my human eyes were straining to see as the sky darkened and the foliage thickened, cutting off the light.

Each step forward was taking me further from my problems, and right now that was good enough for me.

Everything I'd done since leaving Magnus' room would be a disappointment to my pack. Tonight, I'd made one stupid decision after another. I already knew how they would list out each and every one of my sins.

They would see it all as a mistake—but it was *mine* to make. This was the very first mistake I'd allowed myself to make in my life. I didn't need to care about the pressure that the pack put on me. It didn't matter, now. My pack wasn't *here*.

It felt *liberating*.

I could feel it in the air, the moment that I left the Stonevalley territory... I'd never left the territory before. They said that it was too dangerous... that there were things happening to the shifters that left on their own. Something causing lone wolves to disappear.

But they had already dealt with that, right? It ended up being humans after all. Didn't another pack take them down? So, there wasn't anything to worry about. Except maybe ending up facing another shifter pack that hated the Stonevalley wolves.

But I'd been careful. I made sure to avoid other shifter territories. Right now I was running straight into the heart of the unclaimed zone.

Where I'd go from here, that was a problem for the future. All I knew was that the pressure to be with Magnus was crushing me... I couldn't stay. The walls of the Stonevalley castle were closing in and I needed to get out. Before everything that I am, and everything that I wanted for myself was crushed under everyone's expectations.

One second, I was running through the forest and the next I was jerked off my feet, knees scraping across uneven roots and splitting open. My palms slammed hard against the ground, taking the brunt of the impact—a sudden sharp pain flared in my wrist. I tried shaking it off, stopping when it only made it hurt worse.

I rose to my feet slowly, on uneven footing—one of my shoes had slid off my foot when I fell.

What the hell was that?

I hadn't tripped on anything. No. It felt like something had slammed into my leg mid stride, knocking me over.

My gaze darted across my surroundings... but it was so dark. I drew on my wolf, my eyes warming as the cones and rods within them shifted, and immediately the gloom sharpened into focus.

At once, I saw the... thing that tripped me.

Goddess, what is *that?*

It looked like a human, but there was no way that it could be... it was way too skeletal, bones clearly visible in its threadbare and dirty gown. Whatever it was didn't move like a human, its spindly little limbs were crouched like a spider, approaching me slowly in twitchy movements.

Long and matted hair hung over its bony face, hiding eyes that were human shaped but all wrong. They were solid black all over like a demon. But even without the whites of its eyes, I could tell that its gaze was locked on me. With a look that was distinctly *hungry*. Predatory. Moving ever closer in those small and twitchy motions, like I was nothing but a little insect trapped in its web.

Oh, *hell* no.

I called for my wolf, opening up the connection between us, like reaching a mental hand deep within my body to the animal within me, to pull her to the surface... her returning howl came from deep within me... too deep, too soft.

Not at all like the call I'd grown used to ever since I'd come of age. Robust and hearty and willing to burst through my skin. Especially now, so close to the full moon, normally my wolf would be prowling close to my skin, jumping for the chance to tear free.

She was whining frantically, sensing my distress. Why wouldn't she come?

I took one uncertain step back and the thing leapt—so fast that I could barely track it. It would have landed on me if I hadn't jerked out of the way. My first sailed through empty air—I should have made contact. Should have at least grazed it with the claws that burst out my fingertips, only to slice through empty air.

The creature moved inhumanly fast. It launched back to the tree, bony limbs gripping on to the branches, before striking again. Hurtling toward me, open mouthed, with pointed teeth like daggers.

Oh, *fucking shit.*

Why hadn't I recognized the thing as a vampire until its teeth were halfway to my throat?

But they weren't supposed to be here. Vampires would never go into wolf territory, they weren't that stupid. Everything I'd heard about them suggested that they avoided shifter territory for dozens of miles.

But you aren't in shifter territory.

Instinctively, I darted back, though my one lone heel dug into the earth, nearly knocking me off balance.

It wasn't far enough.

Pain. White-hot and searing, ripped through my shoulder.

I turned my head to see those demonic eyes, half-lidded in pleasure, right there. On me. Piercing through my skin, needle-like teeth sinking straight over the celestial pattern of my soulmark—there was something about seeing this *leech,* cutting straight into my bond, slurping at it, that made me see red.

I bashed my fist against its head. Hard. But all I managed to do was make those needle-like teeth sink deeper into me. I could feel it sucking deep. The vampire's dark eyes were shining with greed, gulping away. No matter how many times I hit it, slashed at it with my claws, nothing phased it. It was like the vampire couldn't even feel me pummeling it at all.

Until my arms started to feel heavy and my punches started to weaken.

I'd already run for so long... I was so *tired.*

No.

This wasn't happening... this wasn't supposed to... I wasn't even sure if I'd even wanted to run away. I'd just panicked. I needed some time to think. To get away from the crushing pressure...

I clenched my eyes shut, gritting my teeth against the piercing burn of its teeth. Nothing I did helped. My struggles weakened as the world began to spin, and black spots flitted across my vision.

It fucking *hurt,* and I just wanted it to stop.

"Magnus," I whimpered.

The moment that his name escaped my lips, I knew that running had been a mistake.

He can't hear me now... he can't save me.

What was I doing out here? Vulnerable, away from the safety of the pack? I was going to die here. All alone, because I didn't know how to stop being afraid of my mate.

Why did I only realize that I wanted Magnus more than I feared him now—when it was too late?

CHAPTER 18

MAGNUS

I'd never run faster in my life. The world blurred past me as I ignored the burn in my legs, the pounding of the earth beneath my paws. Never had my wolf and human self been so aligned as now. My human self was just as ferocious, pushing the wolf to *move*. To go. Faster. Nothing mattered except that I had to get to her. Now. Before it was too late.

I was an arrow unleashed, whistling across the grass. Following the ache in my chest, the raw longing in my soul-bond pulled me toward her.

I burst around a thick undergrowth, and the sweet smell of my mate burst across my nostrils, drenched and stricken through with the iron tang of her blood and the sour acid of her fear.

She wasn't alone.

The rancid stench of old blood clogged my nostrils before I saw the *thing* lodged onto her shoulder, teeth jammed straight into the delicate skin of my mate's shoulder... tearing straight into the lovely swirls and constellations that marked our bond.

Vampire.

It must have been starving to venture so close to shifter territory. Should have been more cautious... taking blood from the woman under *my* protection. The second it touched Kira, it was as good as dead.

I would enjoy watching life fade from its eyes.

The parasite didn't even notice me, making no effort to dislodge itself from Kira as I ran behind it, sinking my teeth through its thin neck. The vampire's blood lust didn't let up —the monster was completely fixated. It continued to drink even as my teeth severed through muscle skin and bone. Even completely decapitated, the dirty pest didn't even realize it was dead. Staying lodged deep into her veins, mouth moving like it was continuing to suck.

I tugged at the lanky hair, trying to dislodge it, and noticed that even that little movement was jarring the teeth, cutting into Kira's skin. This was too delicate for my wolf's paws and teeth.

The moment I recognized it, my wolf was already releasing control, drawing back within me. Fur sucked back into my skin like a child slurping spaghetti as my bones shifted, snapping in places, yielding my human form to me.

The moment wolf's paws became human hands again, I carefully pried the vampire's head up, pulling until the teeth broke free from Kira's shoulder with an audible pop. I kept pulling, dislocating bone and ripping through skin until the creature's lower jaw came free. I tossed the pieces of its head away from us, into the bushes.

I didn't even savor the kill. There was no time.

Kira slumped over, losing her footing completely—I had to leap forward to catch her before she fell to the ground.

Her skin was cool to the touch.

I reached for her pulse point, pressing against her soft skin, feeling for her heartbeat, as my own blood pounded through my veins.

I found one. Thank all the gods, Kira was alive. I hadn't been too late.

But it was weak... feebly pulsing beneath my fingertips. I had to think. Had to help her.

There was something wrong with her scent. Something like high pitched static in her blood. It had to be a nasty bit of work that the vampire left behind in her system.

If I could just get her to shift—wolves on the battlefield could be clinging to a scrap of life when they managed to shift. If they were strong enough to manage it, the process would bring them back to their body's peak physical health. Shifting acted like a hard reset on the body, and it might be the only thing that could save her. I only had to wake up the wolf within her.

Holding her gingerly, careful not to make the deep puncture wounds in her shoulder any worse, I shook Kira.

"Baby girl, wake up." Blood that was oddly dark leaked out of her wound as I jostled her.

Her eyes fluttered open—thank the goddess—but her expression was dazed. Hazy and unfocused. She looked right at me and for a moment, it was like she couldn't even recognize me.

"You came." Her voice sounded thick. Slurred. Not at all like her sweet, normal self.

Immediately, my hackles raised. The vampire bite had done something to her, more than just taking blood. Kira sounded like she was drunk.

"Of course I came," I muttered, distracted, as my mind raced through everything I knew about vampires—only to realize I didn't know shit about vampires. Hadn't paid attention to the lessons about them, because they weren't supposed to be a concern.

Vampires generally avoided shifter land. They weren't a threat when our kind was in the wolf form. Their bite was toxic to humans and shifters both. What kind of poison did they release into my mate's blood? What did that thing do to her? Would this bite mean that she was going to turn into one of those things?

Kira reached for me, softly brushing her delicate fingers in a line down my chest.

Her pupils darkened with desire, completely locked on my body. She was staring at me like she needed me to breathe. Like she wanted nothing else. Instinctively, my body reacted, every muscle bunching and tensing under her touch. I wanted to lean into her, let her explore everything. I was *hers*.

I was a dumbass—Kira was *injured*. Of course *now*, would be the time that Kira decided she wanted to explore my body.

What the fuck was I doing? Now was not the time to be thinking with my dick.

I grabbed her hand, halting her progress as her touches drifted lower.

"You're injured. You need to shift." I threw every inch of alpha authority I had into the words. I wasn't her alpha, not the alpha of any pack, but I was dominant enough that her wolf should respond to the command.

Except that nothing happened.

Kira's nose scrunched in concentration, and then she shook her head. "Can't."

Why couldn't she shift? Was this a result of the vampire bite? Or was she just disoriented?

"Kira, you need to try. Shift for me." The words were a command. Sharp and authoritative. Impossible to ignore.

But my alpha commands did nothing... if she was able to shift, she would have done it already. Maybe she would have even shifted into a wolf when she'd seen the creature for the first time.

Something was wrong.

...if Kira couldn't shift.

My gaze lingered on the brutal holes slicing into my mate's soft skin... still oozing blood. How she smelled wrong. Acidic. She was a chemical cocktail of cortisol and the trace of wrongness of whatever the vampire had dumped into her blood.

It felt like the earth was ripped out from under my feet and I was in free-fall.

If Kira couldn't shift, there was nothing stopping this.

Nothing to stem whatever poison the vampire had pumped into her. Nothing to stop her blood as it continued to leak out of her. Nothing to speed up her pulse that had gotten dangerously low and weak.

I needed to get her to a hospital.

Now.

She needed professional medical care, and I couldn't think about what was going to happen to her if she didn't get it. No, I had to focus. I couldn't start panicking.

The closest hospital was human—and that was out of the question. It was one lesson that teachers always drilled into us during training: don't forget how often human hospitals used silver. The deadly metal could be in anything and everything in a human hospital. They used it in their surgical tools and needles, in the bandages and even in their ointments.

The humans said that silver has antibacterial properties, and maybe it does. There is every possibility that it helps heal them faster. It was just too bad that silver is worse than poison for a shifter.

Silver dug straight into the bond between the wolf and man, disrupting the connection that we have with the moon. The wolf within us was more than a spirit that shared our soul—it was a beastly reflection of our true selves. My wolf was the twin to my human self, and as much a part of me as my hands and arms and elbows.

Prolonged contact with silver could drive away and even destroy the wolf within us completely. That destruction wasn't something that a shifter could survive.

Taking Kira to the human hospitals was as good as a death sentence. I had to get her to a shifter hospital.

Honestly, the care that Kira would receive back at the Stonevalley castle wasn't much better. I'd seen a murky glass jar labeled *leeches* in the infirmary... next to the vials of crushed herbs and an old lancet that had been used for blood-letting for over a century. I hadn't cared much that our traditional ways were hopelessly outdated... until now, when it mattered. When our primitive tools were all that stood between Kira and the poison coursing through her veins.

If she even survived the trip back to our territory.

I knew what her best option was—a shifter hospital forbidden for the Stonevalley wolves.

Her eyes were heavy, drifting shut as if she was going to fall back asleep.

Fuck, my mate was losing consciousness.

I jostled her again, grimacing as blood leaked out of her shoulder, trickling down the marks of her soulbond. Kira whimpered softly, and the sound of it pierced me. Even if I did it because I had to, I hated to be the cause of her pain.

"Just hold on," I whispered to her, urgently.

Goddess above, was my mate going to die here in my arms? While I held her and did *nothing*.

Fuck, why wasn't I there to protect her? Why couldn't I have moved faster? This had all happened when I was fucking sleeping.

Berating myself wasn't going to solve anything. I had to *move*. Now. It was the only thing that could save her.

Fuck the consequences. The only thing that mattered was saving her. I could deal with the fallout for my mad escape. I didn't even care if the Alpha's heir deemed it as abandoning the pack.

Nothing mattered, so long as my mate lived.

CHAPTER 19

MAGNUS

My mate in my arms was a time bomb. Her pulse was softly ticking away—so faintly every moment felt like it could be the last.

Once I'd realized she was in danger, I ran to her with nothing. After shifting back from my wolf form, I didn't even have clothes to staunch the bleeding. I sliced one wolf's claw through the thin material of her skirt, slicing off a chunk of fabric, wadding it up and pressing it to her wound.

With Kira in my arms, I ran through the woods, towards forbidden territory. There was every chance that they would shoot me on sight. But I would take the chance of my death over the certainty of hers.

Everyone knew that the best medical care available for shifters was at the Edgeriver pack hospital. The Stonevalley pack and Edgeriver pack had been at war for generations. Technically, that war had ended when the alphas traded their first born children. Hell, when the alpha's heir ended up as the soulmate of the river girl, it cemented the treaty in blood ties.

But that treaty had never been tested.

I was putting both packs at risk. One wrong move on my part, one misunderstanding and war could break out. Even knowing that didn't slow my pace at all, as I sprinted through the forest with Kira limp in my arms.

I would risk everything for her. Burn all the treaties down—if it meant that she could live.

I ran through the uncharted zone, not slowing until I reached the river that marked the edge of their territory.

The River wolves are not our enemies... not technically. Not anymore.

This is exactly why I held back from getting anywhere near Kira.

Deep down, I knew myself. I knew that once I fell for her, there wasn't anything I wouldn't do. No line I wouldn't cross. All for her.

But even though I tried to hold myself back, the moon goddess gave her to me anyway. It seemed like destiny had other plans for me.

Now that I had her, it was too late. I would do *anything* to keep her.

Death couldn't fucking have her. Kira was mine.

I adjusted my grip around her, holding her high out of the path of the cold river water as I waded through. She whimpered, but besides that didn't make a sound. She was too quiet.

The water was piercing cold, but luckily it was moving sluggishly. I forced myself to move, to push through to the other side, even as the cold sapped away at my strength, biting at every inch of my skin.

I held Kira over my head as I crossed over the middle of the river, the depths of rushing water clinging to me. Wading slowly, despite the bitter cold, forcing myself to ignore the tug of the cold water. Forcing myself forward, step after step, through water so cold it *burned.*

When I finally, *finally,* took a step on dry land, and made the mistake of relaxing somewhat, maybe thinking that the worst was over. I'd gotten Kira to medical help—that's when the guard who must have been watching me the entire time I'd struggled through the river, let themself be known.

"Give me one good reason why I shouldn't shoot this arrow through your throat." His arrow was cocked. Even if I couldn't recognize the glint of deadly metal, I knew from our reports that the River guards used silver in their arrow tips—with one twitch of his finger, I was a dead man.

Tearing my gaze away from the arrow notched and poised to kill me, I recognized him, though I had never stepped foot on River territory before. I'd seen his same face every time I delivered reports and took orders: the guard before me was Erik Decoteau, but that was not always his name. As the eldest of the alpha's twin sons, he had been born Erik Ragnolf.

In an effort to put a stop to the endless war, the alphas of the Stonevalley and Edgeriver packs exchanged their firstborn children. Before the treaty, before the trade, *he* was the alpha who would have taken over the Stonevalley pack.

Now he was the shifter with the silver-tipped arrow, armed and ready to kill me.

This man, with the face of our alpha's heir—his exact features, here on the other side of the river, looked like he had no sympathy for the pack who'd raised him. The calm look on his face made it clear that if I didn't give him a good enough reason, I was a dead man. This man was no longer Aaron Ragnolf's brother. The only thing that the two of them had in common would be the disgust with me that they had to both be experiencing, for leaving my territory behind and ending up where I clearly was not meant to be.

Within me, my wolf was pacing, recognizing the dominance in the older wolf. If we had to take him on in a fight, I could already sense the outcome. Could already sniff out the power in the other wolf, the dominance in his bloodline.

And with Kira? Defenseless at my side?

I had no chance of taking him on if I wanted to defend her. Hell, even if I managed to fight like the devil and overpower this wolf, how long would it take? How long did she even have left?

"Please," the word felt foreign on my tongue. I didn't beg. As a dominant wolf, I'd never had to... But I had no pride when it came to Kira's safety. The threat of her dying had ripped my ego wide open. I had to keep her safe.

I couldn't live without her.

"It's my mate. She's dying." My voice was steady, but I could feel my blood race as I admitted out loud what was happening to the woman in my arms—the woman who had long mattered more to me than my own life.

From the moment I saw her, it was as if my heart had been ripped out of me. I didn't know about the organ beating in my chest, because my heart was *here* in my arms. This fragile little thing that I needed more than the blood flowing through my veins.

She couldn't die.

Erik glared at me. His gaze was stone cold. His fingers twitched on the bow, as if he would like nothing more than to strike me down.

"A dominant wolf like you is nothing but trouble. What if I tell you the only way that I'd think about letting your mate into my territory is if she gets in over your dead body?"

"If it means that my mate gets to live, do it." I raised my chin, offering him a clear shot.

Erik cocked his head to the side in a wolfish gesture. His nostrils flared wide as he took in our scent. Testing the truth of my words and sniffing out any lies on his own.

He wouldn't find any. I'd never been more honest in my life.

I held his gaze, refusing to back down. I had to... I didn't care if Erik decided that the best thing for his pack was to strike me down... so long as he stepped over my corpse to provide Kira with the help that she needed... it was Kira's only chance.

Erik shook his head even as he lowered his bow.

"Why is it that every expectant Stone wolf wants to waltz through our territory?" he muttered.

What did that even mean?

But whatever nonsense he was saying didn't matter, for Erik had turned his back on me and was walking away. My wolf snarled quietly in my chest. It was a grave insult for a shifter to turn his back on another fighter, but I ignored it. Erik Decoteau was allowing us into River territory.

I shoved my pride aside... I had to. Kira's life depended on it.

CHAPTER 20
MAGNUS

Erik Decoteau led us through the River territory, as if he were a prison guard taking us to jail rather than to their shifter hospital. Unlike the Stonevalley castle, the River wolves lived in clusters of houses, with shared common areas. Erik headed straight through the door of one large wooden cabin. Inside were clean halls, vinyl floors, and the scent of antiseptic. We passed by several rooms with white clipboards labeled "silver sick."

Inhaling deeply, the trace of the deadly metal was an ache in my nostrils. It didn't make sense that so many River wolves had suffered from silver sickness. The pack must have agreed to take them in for treatment.

Once we got to an unoccupied room, I lay Kira down in a bed, pulling up a nearby chair to sit near her. Erik didn't leave us. Instead, he leaned against the wall, casually crossing his arms with a bored look on his face, as if it would be no problem at all for him to reach out for his weapons to murder me if I let my behavior get out of hand. He completely ignored me, acting as if I wasn't even in the room at all. Erik didn't say a word until a young woman in scrubs walked in. His eyes focused on her, following her every movement. As she stopped by him, playfully nudging his elbow, Erik said to her, "Anabella, tell me if this asshole even looks at you wrong."

She nodded, as if she was used to Erik's solemn vows to rain violence down on his enemies—she probably was. Erik didn't have any visible soulmarks on him, and he was practically treating the girl with the kind of attention a dominant wolf reserved only for his mate. Maybe he was just the type that was super protective of women.

Anabella wasted no time placing devices on Kira that I didn't recognize, which hooked up to a machine that started beeping. The air flooded with the harsh scent of disinfectant as she cleaned out Kira's bite wound and covered it with a bandage.

Anabella didn't even flinch as my wolf snarled in my chest, getting agitated as she approached Kira with a needle. I gritted my teeth, mentally soothing my wolf, telling him that this was helping our mate. *It's an IV bag. It'll give back the fluids she lost.*

The beast within me growled as a needle broke through Kira's skin but made no move to wrest control over me to protect her. My wolf trusted my judgment, as I trusted his.

Kira was all hooked up to wires and machines softly beeping. The unfamiliar medical equipment was putting me on edge—it was one thing to know that a different pack had access to modern technology and quite another to see all these machines monitoring her... Kira's life was laid out in beeps and lines flashing across screens.

The doctor strode in from another room, wearing a white overcoat with a stethoscope wrapped around her neck. Her name tag identified her as Dr. Lakeland. "Can you tell me what happened?"

"It was a vampire bite." I was digging my nails into the wood of the chair by her bed, leaving deep grooves from my wolf claws. "What's going to happen? Is she going to turn into one of those... things?"

"Not likely from just a bite."

At the doctor's words, something tight in the pit of my stomach released. I felt like I could breathe again.

But I couldn't fully relax... not with Kira drifting in and out, whining faintly every time someone moved her, to give her more tests, more fluids... trying to figure out what was going on with her body.

Was she going to be okay? What had the venom done to her?

The doctor scanned the machines with a furrow between her eyebrows. "What happened exactly? How did the vampire get to her?"

"I'm not sure, I got there after it happened, and she wasn't making sense after the bite."

"Why didn't she shift?"

I'd been asking myself the exact same question.

"She tried. She said that she couldn't." I shrugged.

I'd actually never seen Kira shift, but it didn't matter. I knew the scent of the wolf within her as intimately as I knew my own. Kira had a wolf, but for some reason she wouldn't come, wouldn't protect her... which didn't make any sense.

Dr. Lakeland tapped an index finger against her cheek, deep in thought. "Hang on," she murmured, giving Anabella a *look* that I didn't like.

Anabella stepped out and came back, rolling in another machine. She went about setting it up, switching on a monitor.

"What is that?" I was wound up tight, being here in another shifter's territory, alone, the only defense for my injured mate... I had to trust the two of these shifters who would have tried ripping me to shreds less than a decade ago just for being on their land. They were the only ones who could help my mate.

Now they definitely knew something that they weren't telling me.

"Just a simple test, it won't hurt her at all." Dr. Lakeland pulled up the hem of Kira's shirt, exposing her lower belly.

Had the vampire's poison shredded her insides? Broken the wolf within my mate?

No, the scent of the wolf was still there. I could smell her—earthy and spiced with the wild, like running through the heart of an old-growth forest.

Then why was the doctor lining up medical equipment on a tray?

Living at the Stonevalley castle meant that I wasn't the most familiar with modern technology. The elder wolves tended to be rather traditional. Obviously, our homes had the obvious modern conveniences like plumbing and basic electricity... but the elders drew the line on things like computers and cellphones.

But I did live in the world. I had gone on enough missions to know what things were, despite the fact that I was never given the same access to things in the way that a non shifter would be exposed to technology.

The doctor held a tool shaped like something that should be able to attach a computer to a monitor, though the end was smooth.

She must have sensed my confusion, because she turned to me to explain, "this is called a transducer probe. This is going to give us a better sense of what is happening in her body." The doctor tried to calm my nerves. "We're just testing out a theory."

Squirting blue gel on the probe, she pressed it against Kira's lower stomach, moving it around. All of a sudden there was a sound of whooshing, and a fast beating... like a horse galloping.

Anabella gasped softly. She and the doctor leaned in, looking at the monitor, pointing at the screen and whispering.

"It looks like the baby's okay."

"Whose baby?" What were they talking about? They needed to focus on Kira right now. On the vampire bite.

"Your mate's fetus..." Dr. Lakeland gestured to the monitor.

There, in a grainy black and white screen... that was a baby. I could make out the tiny features, its huge head, the little bulge of a stomach... the tiny limbs with even tinier fingers and toes. When the probe moved, there was the shadow of the eyes and nose.

Not just any baby. That was *my* baby. It was a biological fact. Kira hadn't been with anyone other than me. Somehow, even after all of those nights with Kira, her legs spread open underneath me... I hadn't made the connection to *this*.

I stared at Kira's flat belly underneath the probe. I hadn't noticed anything different at all. Hadn't noted a change in her scent. Not in her body or in any of her behaviors.

She was pregnant. I'd gotten my mate pregnant.

A brief image of Kira, with her belly swollen with my child flashed through my mind. Carrying my child. Mine. My claim on her—there for everyone to see. So everyone who saw her would know that I fucked her so hard that I left a part of myself behind and growing within her... hot desire, like lightning shot all the way down my spine.

Wait.

I had to stop thinking with my dick for a second, at least *once* over the course of my relationship.

Oh. *Shit.*

Kira had panicked after I told her I love her... how was she going to react when she found out she was pregnant with my baby?

"We've only been together for three months, though."

"Really? The fetus is measuring at three months—at the bare minimum."

"Well, yeah. We uhh..." This was awkward as fuck. The last thing I wanted was to talk about how I'd soulbonded with my mate and immediately taken her off to some dark corner and fucked her. Apparently, I'd done more than that —I'd impregnated her too. Or maybe it was the next day, when all I'd done was her. In her bed. Making her come over and over again. "I thought that it took longer for shifters?"

None of the shifters in the Stonevalley pack were really getting pregnant—except for the alpha's heir. He'd had a kid. Besides that though, no one had gotten pregnant in the pack, not in a *decade*. It's not like the wolves in the pack were abstinent, either. The smell of sex was all over the dark corners and disused classrooms in the castle. I'd always heard people say that it often took years, sometimes even decades, for shifter women to conceive.

"It only takes one time. Even with shifters." Dr. Lakeland moved the probe even lower, maneuvering it around. "See there, there she is."

On the screen, right below my baby, there was a large shadow in the shape of the wolf. That was Kira's shifter self, within her body, curled protectively around our child. As I watched, the wolf lifted her head up from over her paws and showed her teeth in a growl. As if she knew that she was being watched.

"Some wolves are just more maternal than others. They refuse to do anything that'll put the little ones at risk. It's actually a pretty reliable indicator for shifter pregnancy. If the she-wolf won't shift, it could be a sign that she's protecting her unborn child. Oh—"

Kira's wolf took a swipe at the probe, jostling the image on the monitor. I could actually see her belly move as the wolf inside of her took offense.

"Well, that explains why she wasn't shifting. Your mate's wolf is extremely protective of her little one. Let's give her some space for now." The doctor suggested, flipping off the monitor. She took a towel and wiped the remnants of the gel off Kira's stomach.

Okay, we'd deal with... *this*... later.

First, I needed to make sure that Kira was okay. She was still bitten by a freaking bloodsucking *vampire,* whatever else was happening inside of her body.

"Alright, besides the fact that I knocked her up, is she going to be okay?" This had all happened because of me. If I could have just held it together, and not scared her off by telling her that I was in love with her, none of this would have happened.

"She's lost a lot of blood, and her blood pressure is low. She'll need to rest..." Dr. Lakeland rearranged some papers that did not look like they needed to be rearranged, breaking eye contact with me. "Then there's the venom to deal with. Are you aware of the side effects of vampire venom?"

I shook my head, bracing myself for the worst.

The doctor nodded, looking uncomfortable. "Vampire venom tends to cause an increase of arousal in its victims.

That will probably stay in her system and cause some disorientation for the next couple of hours."

So my mate was going to wake up... really horny?

"Yeah, I'm not staying for that," Erik muttered from where he stood silently brooding against the wall. He turned to leave, signaling for Anabella to follow him out. Erik glared at me one last time over his shoulder.

"If you cause any trouble for my pack, I'll still kill you."

CHAPTER 21

MAGNUS

Kira slept, peacefully unaware, even as the doctor slipped in to check on her vitals and took out her IV line.

According to the doctor, she was doing better. She just needed rest. Then the doctor bombarded me with new vitamins Kira was supposed to be taking, printed out photos of her fetus and a list of foods and activities that were forbidden to her now.

How was Kira going to react to all this? She didn't even want to acknowledge me in public. I couldn't assume that she was going to be okay with this.

I had an uncomfortable question and as much as I hated it, I had to ask.

"What if she doesn't react well to the news? What are her options?"

The doctor's face fell as she worked out what I was implying. "Well, if she didn't want it, shifting at this stage would likely end in miscarriage, unless the fetus is a strong enough shifter themselves to survive the transformation in utero. But honestly," the doctor gave me a between-you-

and-me look, "the wolf's desires often align with their human self. If the wolf is this maternal, I don't see your mate wanting to end this pregnancy."

Okay. According to the doctor, Kira was going to want this to happen. This was happening.

I didn't know anything about babies.

I hadn't seen any of them around the Stonevalley castle, besides the Heir's baby, Leo, who was kept under strict supervision. A general like me had no reason to be in close proximity to the alpha heir's son. Especially as it was getting clearer to everyone that while the old alpha still lived, he wasn't the one who held the power. The alpha's heir took on all the full responsibilities of the pack. He was the alpha in all but name, making little Leo the pack's true heir.

Children were completely out of my realm of experience... All I knew was that they were delicate and vulnerable. It was a little terrifying to think about that level of responsibility, keeping a little one like that alive.

I stared down at Kira sleeping—her wavy hair like cascading strands of honey.

I love her. With everything in me, I love her.

This baby was a part of her. How could I do anything but love the little one too?

An hour later, Kira woke up.

Her deep blue eyes flickered open. She glanced around the room until her gaze landed on me.

I didn't miss how her pupils bloomed dark with desire. Her lovely little pink tongue darted out, wetting her lips. I couldn't help but follow every single motion of it. Kira's pouting lips parted and she pressed toward me in a devastating invitation.

She was magnetic; I was helplessly drawn into her orbit.

"Magnus," Kira whimpered.

She reached out to me, her fingers brushed against my arm, sensuously. The heat of her touch was driving me wild.

But I remembered the words of the doctor. *Vampire venom tends to cause an increase in arousal in its victims.*

I had to remember that Kira was a victim.

She wasn't in her right mind.

Internally groaning, I shook my head. I leaned away from Kira to put some space between us. I reached for her hand on my arm, holding her back from the torturous trails she was weaving across my body. "If you still want me in the morning, I'll be all yours."

Kira's voice wavered, as she forced out words that were slurred like she was drunk. "I need you. It hurts."

Well, shit.

Obviously, I wasn't about to let her be in pain.

I leaned in, taking in those deep blue eyes that were like falling straight into the depths of the ocean. Eyes that widened with desire as she watched me. Kira was so gorgeous, and she needed me.

But what if she woke up the next morning, and she hadn't really wanted this? I'd always been able to tell before by her scent that she was aroused. But that was before Kira had run from me. What if she felt violated by intimacy right now, under the influence of vampire venom? I couldn't take advantage of her.

"Please." Her eyes were red rimmed, filled with unshed tears.

I had to help her. She needed me. There was no way in hell that I was going to let her feel rejected when she needed me so bad, that it *hurt*.

I pushed Kira down flat on the bed and had to pause to get myself under control as she gasped. As I tore down her pants and underwear, she whimpered so sweetly. My borrowed pants were still firmly buckled—even though my cock was hard and throbbing for her. I ignored it.

This was about *her*.

I got to my knees at the foot of her infirmary bed with her luscious thighs on either side of me, bracketing my ears. I grabbed Kira by her hips, pulling her to the edge of the bed. Moving closer to her glistening pussy, I watched her ocean blue eyes widen and her lips part as she realized what I was about to do.

Kira was practically dripping for me. Her gorgeous little cunt was open and on display, all swollen and flushed red. Her needy little clit was hooded and standing at attention. My girl was so ready. So perfect.

I needed more of her, needed to be closer.

It started with a kiss against the heated flesh of her pussy...

Oh, *fuck*.

Her taste burst across my tongue, musky and sweeter than I could have ever imagined.

Why hadn't I ever done this before?

I dove straight in, pressing my tongue in deeper, needing more of her, needing to taste her, needing her more than I needed anything. She was my air, my life, my everything.

The moment I touched her, Kira's back arched and she moaned. I slid my tongue deeper into her core, and she whimpered, her eyes hazy with lust. Kira spread her legs wider, opening herself up more for me. I lapped at her sweetness, letting her juices drip down my chin.

Kira rode my face, her hips wild against me as she sought her pleasure. I matched each of her desperate movements as her hips thrust harder against my mouth. I suckled, and drank her, fucking her with my tongue until Kira's fingers were gripping my hair, holding me in place.

As if anything on the goddess' green earth would make me leave this pussy now.

I wasn't stopping until I felt her shatter all around me. At least twice.

Kira was keening, wild and uninhibited. Moaning out my name desperately. I reached out and grabbed her hand, steadying her and telling her without words that I was here. I wasn't going to stop.

My mate's moans were guttural and raw with need. She bucked frantically, seeking out that little bit of pressure to tip her over the edge.

She seemed so close. Hovering right over the precipice and just needing that one little push to tip her over.

I put my mouth directly over her swollen clit and sucked down.

Hard.

She arched her back, groaning helplessly as she came.

Kira's thighs that were around my shoulders began to shake with the force of it.

I pressed my tongue against her, not letting up the pressure right where she needed it. I was determined to stretch this out for her... wanted her to feel it.

This was about her... and I would do everything in my power to make sure that this was good for her, to stretch out each and every moment of her pleasure.

She deserved everything, every bit of bliss I could wring out of her.

For as long as she needed me, I would do this over and over again. Happy to help my mate ease *all* of the vampire's venom out of her system.

I looked into Kira's lovely eyes as she came down from the highs of her orgasm—ocean eyes that were half lidded in pleasure. Her chest rose and fell, making her perfect tits jiggle slightly as she caught her breath.

The only thing I could do was silently swear to the moon goddess...

Even knowing that I had done nothing to deserve this... after I had fucked everything up. If I got another chance to make things right with my mate, I was going to do whatever it took to be the man I should have been for her from the very beginning.

I was finally here, right where she needed me.

Now that I had gotten a real taste of her, nothing was going to keep my stubborn ass from fighting for her.

CHAPTER 22
KIRA

I woke up and saw Magnus' warm gray eyes, staring down at me. I blushed as I remembered last night, and how he had taken care of me like he had never taken care of me before.

I'd never felt so wanton, so out of control. It was like I was drunk—I was powerless under the force of my desire. The things that usually held me back, didn't matter anymore. My pride didn't matter, or my worries about my past with Magnus. None of it mattered, but what I wanted… I chased after it—relentlessly.

Magnus had been right there when I needed him, and *goddess damn* did he deliver.

I might have been delirious, under the influence of whatever the vampire had done to me, but I remembered everything. Every swipe of Magnus' tongue against my swollen pussy. How his rough hands—his every touch, made my body sing for him.

It was fucking mind blowing.

I'd never felt more free. Not once in my entire life.

It took me a moment to realize that I had no idea where

we were. I was surrounded by beeping machines, and the scents of the area were all wrong. It was antiseptic and something foreign in the air. Was that pine?

"Where are we?" my voice felt hoarse, like I hadn't used it in days.

"We're in the infirmary, at the River territory," Magnus said, not taking his eyes off me.

Wait. The *River* territory. I'd never been so far away from the Stonevalley territory before in my life. This shifter territory wasn't just far from home—being here was forbidden! We weren't currently at war, but after generations of bloodshed between the two packs, it was more than frowned upon to travel between packs. If the others found out about it, we could be shunned. We might not even be allowed back into the pack if the alpha's heir was angry enough about it.

The shock must have shown on my face, because Magnus explained. "You were too far from the Stonevalley pack, and you needed medical attention."

I nodded slowly. That made sense. It was risky, but I understood why he would do it.

He did it for me.

Because he *loves* me, even though hearing that had only led me to run from him... when really after the two of us had gotten together, he hadn't done anything to hurt me. I had waited for three months for the other shoe to drop, for him to revert back to the asshole who was always so quick to hurt me, but that man never showed himself. Only the kind of mate who would drop everything to run after me and keep me safe.

Magnus sighed and ran his hands through his dark hair, mussing it up. The air filled with a scent I hadn't encountered around him before—anxiety, like sour and bitter acid.

I bit my lip as I watched him.

What did he have to be anxious about now? I was feeling a lot better now.

I couldn't help but think back to last night. Magnus hadn't even taken care of his own needs, just soothed the burning away from me, making me feel so good. Magnus was there for me when I had needed him most. He took care of me.

But what if I had gotten it all wrong? What if last night wasn't about giving me what I needed? What if he had just wanted to create space between the two of us?

Was he... mad at me for running away?

It made sense. He'd told me that he loves me and I ran away, off Stonevalley territory straight into the teeth of a vampire. I had nearly gotten myself killed.

It had taken running away and facing down death for me to realize that the only person I wanted was the man that I had once sworn that I would hate forever. I might have seen him as my own personal bully; for much of my life he was my worst enemy. But when it came down to it, when I was alone and afraid, it was *his* name that I whispered in the face of death. *His* handsome face that I wanted to see. I had known deep in the depths of my soul that he would be there for me. Magnus would protect me. He would always protect me.

At that moment, I realized that I wanted him—all of him, past included.

For the first time in my life, as I stared at the undying devotion that burned in his eyes as he looked at me, I felt safe. I wanted the protection that came from a big strong alpha in my corner. I wanted the strength of his arms wrapped around me.

I wanted him—and everything that came with it, all for myself.

Now that I knew what I wanted, was I going to lose it all?

Was I going to lose my soulmate before I even had a chance to really be with him? All because I'd made one stupid, panic driven mistake?

"Baby..." Magnus winced after saying the nickname he'd always used for me. "Kira, we need to talk."

"Okay," the word was barely a whisper. I tried to swallow, to force down some of the anxiety rising up my throat, threatening to choke me.

The tension was heavy in the air around us. The last time I felt like this was the vague impression I'd had when I first learned that my mother was taken down in the battle-field. Faint whispers around me, murmurs about the healers doing everything they could. I remembered hoping and praying as hard as I could, and how none of that made any difference.

"Do you know how the River wolves use more advanced technology?"

I nodded.

I'd never left the Stonevalley territory, but I had heard people talk. I knew the way that we were living in the castle was very traditional. Humans and even other shifters lived very differently. There were whispered talks. People wondered whether things would finally change under the new alpha when the Heir officially took over the pack. But what did that have to do with anything? Why would that cause the shadowed expression on Magnus' face?

"It was part of the reason I was willing to risk taking

you here for treatment. The River wolves have access to healthcare that is decades ahead of the nurse's back at the Stonevalley territory."

What wasn't he saying? It seemed like he was holding things back. I didn't understand where he was going with this. Why the lecture about the differences in our packs? Was he just trying to avoid the conversation between the two of us? Well, he was the one that wanted to bring it up in the first place, so why would he...

"They have the technology to look inside of your body. They did it when they couldn't figure out what was wrong." Magnus trailed off, and he brushed his fingers through his hair again. His dark locks usually looked messy, but never like he had strangled the fluff out of them.

Oh, shit.

They found something.

I got this all wrong. They found something wrong with my body. Something that had Magnus feeling nervous, and I had *never* seen him nervous. Not once in *years* of knowing him, had he acted like anything but his confident self.

Magnus took a deep breath and started over. "The two of us haven't been together for very long. We haven't had the chance to talk about certain things."

The two of us hadn't done a lot of talking at all. Unless any of the communication via body language counted... on his bed and in the abandoned hallways.

Now that we finally started communicating, things were all wrong. Even this conversation was going all over the place. Did this have something to do with the fact that my wolf wouldn't come? What was wrong with my body? Why was Magnus looking at me like he was afraid of what my reaction was going to be?

He was officially scaring me.

I put my hand over his, stopping him. "Tell me."

I had to know whatever it was that had him so scared. I needed him to just spit it out.

"You're pregnant." Magnus was tense as he braced himself for my reaction.

For a moment it was so silent that I'd be able to hear a pin drop.

He was saying... I was what?

"No, I'm not." I would have known if I was pregnant.

I would be like, I don't know, throwing up or something. Or my boobs would hurt, or smells would bother me. Nothing like that had happened. Besides, why would Magnus be the one to know more of what was going on within my body than me? It was *my* body.

Magnus didn't look relieved at all to hear me deny it. Instead he reached into his pocket, pulling out a really grainy black and white picture. I had to stare at it for a minute before I realized that the picture was meant to look like a baby.

Okay? Why was he showing me this?

The hand that wasn't holding the picture had his wolf claws out and digging into the arms of his chair—a chair that already had deep scratches etched into it. "The doctor took a picture. This is called an ultrasound. It's a picture of your womb."

I stared again at the picture—the literal *picture* taken of the inside of me, with a baby growing in it.

There was no way.

I couldn't think. My mind was numb.

"It's why you couldn't shift." Magnus' eyes darted between mine, looking for a sign. For anything. He didn't know that my thoughts were plunged under a frozen lake, and I was drowning.

Until suddenly the picture in his hand made sense, like a stubborn lock finally turning for the key. The picture in his hand stopped looking like grainy black and white static. Those little features, little head and stomach, little fingers —it all coalesced until I was looking at a baby.

Not just a baby. That was *my* baby.

How was this possible?

Well, obviously, I knew *how* I'd gotten pregnant... but I had always heard that it took shifters decades to conceive. It was something that the elder wolves talked about in whispers. I'd seen plenty of the older female shifters in tears, talking about how hard it was, how it just wasn't happening for them.

Honestly, this wasn't on my radar at all.

I was pregnant?

I forced my gaze away from the photo in his hand. It didn't seem possible, but somehow it was.

Magnus and I were going to have a baby.

My gaze shot to his. Looking at the tense expression on Magnus' face, I went cold for another reason altogether.

Did he not want a baby with me?

I'd gotten so much of this wrong already. Had I gotten this part wrong too?

Was this why Magnus was so stressed? We had never talked about it and now we might be in trouble from the pack because I ran from him... All this time I had been under the impression that Magnus would be more than happy for the two of us to go public with our relationship. Between the two of us, I was the one who had wanted to hide our soulbond.

But none of that meant that Magnus wanted a child with me. Maybe he only wanted me for sex. He was a high-ranking wolf after all, and it was hard to find a lower-ranking wolf than me. I sat with the gamma wolves, the furthest from the seat of power as it was possible to go. Maybe Magnus had always intended to have his offspring with someone higher up in the pack hierarchy. Someone that suited him better.

I could picture the life that my child would have in the pack if the little one was rejected by their father.

I knew exactly what it felt like to grow up unwanted.

How the eyes of the other adults would glaze over me, as if I didn't even exist.

The way it felt when none of the other kids really wanted to play with me. Even when I did manage to make myself a friend, as soon as their parents saw them playing with me, they would suddenly drift away without any explanation.

I knew what it was like knowing that no matter what I did, it would never be enough. I had lost my place... my brother fought against it for years, tooth and nail.

But that wasn't me. I was always drowning under the weight of it. It was too much pressure for me to try my everything, desperately fighting for begrudging acceptance.

Was... that going to happen to my child as well?

As soon as it clicked in my mind that I was pregnant, something shifted within me. It was like something vulnerable within me was brutally ripped wide open, and all that was left was raw determination.

I knew what it was like to feel barely tolerated by your pack. For years I'd endured it... saying that it was for my brother's sake. I let everyone look down on me, communicating with their cold indifference exactly the place I had in the pack.

I tolerated it for years... but this little one growing inside me?

There was no way in hell I'd let my child deal with that.

I shook my head, trying to control my spiraling thoughts. Here I was already considering the pros and cons of moving to different packs... thinking about whether or not my brother would consider leaving with me... and I hadn't even finished talking to Magnus yet. I hadn't even heard him say that he didn't want this child.

The two of us had never communicated properly. That had to change now. Even if it was just for the last time.

"Do you not want to have a baby with me?"

CHAPTER 23
MAGNUS

Fuck.

How the hell had I fucked everything up past the point of recognition, until my soulmate was staring at me like she was barely holding back tears, thinking that I would abandon her after getting her pregnant?

How had I fucked up this royally? From the very beginning between the two of us, it was like I couldn't ever get on the path to make the right decisions.

I wasn't going to let her think that I didn't want her. Not for another second.

That ended now.

I sprung forward, grabbing Kira and wrapping my arms around her, like holding her could somehow erase all the distance between us. Kira had been calm a moment ago when asking me if I was going to abandon her, as if it wouldn't socially destroy her, but here in my arms, I felt her shaking.

My mate could be so brave, but she didn't have to be. Not anymore. Not when she had me to be brave for her. I wasn't going to let her go until she knew in her bones that I would always protect her.

My confession poured from me.

"I've fucked all of this up. From the beginning. Even before the two of us ever got together, I was already fucking it all up... when all this time you have been the only person I've ever wanted. I never should have treated you the way I'd treated you."

I held Kira's delicate face in my hands, staring into her ocean eyes which were turning red as they filled with unshed tears. "I'm sorry."

I never should have pushed her away from me. Never should have given her a reason to fear me... Kira. The one woman who I'd always longed for. The one woman who I would have given anything to have and instead brutally pushed away.

"It's always been you. I've been in love with you for most of my life, and I didn't know how to handle it." There it was, the truth that I should have told her long ago... finally pouring out my reluctant lips, because Kira deserved to know.

"If you love me, then...why?" Kira whispered.

I didn't need to ask her for clarification. I knew exactly what she meant. If I loved her, why did I push her away? If I loved her, why did I save every cutting remark, every criticism, every bit of nastiness I could muster all for her?

How could I tell her that it was because I wanted her so badly that every inch of my body was tense with the pain of it? That my desire for her was boiling me alive? All I wanted was her and the thought that I would never have her was driving me to raging violence. That if I had ever seen anyone touch her, I didn't even know if I would have been able to stop myself. The thought that I would never have her almost killed me.

"I love you and I'm an idiot. I've made nothing but mistakes handling how I feel about you. It's just your rotten luck that you ended up with me, because I have been nothing but stupid about love." I wrapped my arms just a little tighter around her, trying to communicate without words how I never wanted to let her go. How I never would again. "You never should have had to question how I feel about you... because I am hopelessly gone for you. I should have been there defending you... been there for you when you needed me."

I rubbed soothing paths across her back as Kira stopped holding back her tears, letting them soak into the shirt I'd borrowed from the River pack.

My hand drifted down, touching her lower stomach, just below her belly button.

"You lost your family too soon. I'll give you a family. I'll make sure that you never feel alone again."

Tentatively, Kira placed her hand over mine, gently interlocking our fingers over her belly. Right over the exact spot where she was growing our child.

She looked up at me with a silent question in her eyes. Asking me without words, did I really want this?

I pressed a sweet kiss against her cheek, tasting the salt of her tears.

"Anything you want, it's yours."

Magnus was holding me like I was precious to him.

Being wrapped up in his arms somehow made all of my worries melt away. Without him saying a word, it felt like everything was going to be alright. He was just so big and strong. Magnus' solid presence soothed all my worries away.

Pressing my hand to my belly, I whispered. "So you're not mad about this?"

I froze a bit... I meant to just think that, I hadn't even meant to say it out loud.

It was just such a jarring shift from thinking that he didn't want a future with me, to the thought that Magnus was going to be there for me. It was hard to get my head around what my heart had been whispering to me this whole time...

Magnus was mine.

My mate shook his head, then leaned closer to me. His voice got husky and deep as he whispered, "If you weren't pregnant but you wanted to be, I'd fuck a baby into you right now."

Well, *damn.*

Every thought in my head turned into the consistency of goo, as his sexy voice made me melt inside.

So that answered my question about how Magnus felt about raising a family with me.

But I still had messed everything up by panicking and running away. We were still in enemy territory. Both of us had left our pack without permission. If we returned to the pack, there was always the chance that they wouldn't allow our return.

"What if the Heir doesn't let us go back?" I leaned into Magnus' chest, just enjoying the feeling of his strong arms around me. "Where do we go now?"

"We could stay here if you want." Magnus shrugged. "I've heard some of the younger shifters say that if they could get past the River stench, they wouldn't mind living in this pack."

"What do the Edgeriver wolves have that we don't?"

"Cellphones."

"What are those?"

"Machines that people can talk to others with... but I heard they mostly use them to play games."

Well that sounded rather pointless. I wasn't a child, and didn't need any little machines for games. Not that I was going to say that.

Things still felt too raw and new with Magnus. We were only just tentatively starting to really communicate with one another. This was the first time that we were treating each other like a real couple.

It almost felt like it was too good to last. Like if I said something too weird, it would break the illusion, or this truce between the two of us, and the Magnus that was my devoted lover, would evaporate like the morning dew, leaving behind nothing but the bully who had treated me like crap for my entire life.

Maybe later I would feel comfortable around him— maybe when it wasn't just an hour after I learned that I was knocked up and on enemy territory.

"I don't want to leave my brother," I admitted.

For most of my life, my brother was all that I had. While Sylas might have fought to work his way through the ranks of the pack, he had never once thought of abandoning me to my lower status. He might have hated it, but he always stuck by me.

I couldn't just leave Sylas behind now.

The choice might have been taken out of my hands the moment I'd decided to run... but I had to know if this could be salvaged.

Would I abandon my own flesh and blood in order to play some childish games on the River wolves' fancy phone technology?

Obviously not.

Magnus nodded in agreement. "As soon as the doctor clears you for traveling, we'll head back to the Stonevalley territory."

"But what if the Heir doesn't let us come back?"

Magnus kissed my forehead gently. "Then we'll figure it out."

I FULLY HAD the intention to just talk to Magnus.

I don't know what it was about this man, but whenever I was around him, talking was never enough. One moment I was staring at his plush lips and then the two of us were kissing. His lips were soft and inviting. Each time his mouth pressed against mine, a jolt of electricity shot down the length of my spine. Then his tongue was teasing the edge of my lower lip and I was opening up for him.

He felt so fucking good... his touches lit me on fire until I would burn apart without him.

Magnus was everything I ever wanted... everything I never even knew that I needed.

It wasn't enough. I needed more of him. The scent of his arousal was surrounding me, spicy-sweet, and I wanted to drown in it. I needed him to sink inside of me, until he was everywhere.

A soft knock at the door had me tearing away from him like some naughty child caught with their hand in the cookie jar.

The doctor, a tall proud woman with long dark hair, paused before entering the room. I know that she could smell the hazy scent of desire hanging over the two of us, and I didn't even need to see her nostrils flare for it to be obvious that she knew exactly what we were on the verge of doing.

She cleared her throat. "Is now a good time?"

Magnus looked on the verge of saying no, and going right back to ravishing me, even with the good doctor able to hear everything that we were doing through the thin walls. So I cut in and replied, "yes."

My voice was only a little bit high-pitched, almost on the verge of squeaky.

It was a pity—I had survived a vampire attack only to

die here on enemy territory... of pure embarrassment.

She came into the room, rolling in a bit of equipment with a monitor and probes attached. "Let's see if your wolf will let you get a good look." The doctor flipped the machine on and lifted up the hem of my shirt. She squirted a glob of blue gel right onto my lower belly.

From somewhere deep, *deep*, within me, I could hear my wolf growling.

I reached down to my connection to the wolf, whispering to her.

The doctor is *helping* our little one. Checking to see if they are healthy.

Let her work.

I could feel that my wolf didn't like hearing that. She was so tense, with her hackles raised and ready to fight if she didn't like the look of anything the doctor did. But my wolf allowed the doctor to place the end of her little machine on my stomach. Though she made it very clear to me that she didn't like this at all.

Any sign that this thing was going to harm her pup and she would put a quick end to the machine and to the doctor controlling it.

I stared at my flat stomach doubtfully. Everyone around me seemed convinced... the doctor, Magnus, my own damn *wolf*. But my belly didn't look any different to me. My waist was rather small and there wasn't even a bump or anything. I wasn't even sure how a baby was supposed to fit inside there at all.

But then on the screen, there in black and white was that same image of a little fetus. Now its little arms were huddled close to its body. I could see the little legs moving.

The doctor shifted the probe around on my belly, getting different angles. She took a close look at all the fingers and toes and everything, maneuvering the probe to see the little one from various angles.

"Do you want to know the gender?" The doctor asked all at once.

I swallowed.

She could tell already? I'd barely even had time to wrap my head around everything. It still didn't feel like this was actually happening. It was more like listening to a story about someone's distant relative than a change inside my own body.

It was only by the way that my eyes were glued to the monitor, leaning forward as close as I could go that left me to realize that yes, I wanted to know.

Wordlessly, I nodded.

"You have a little girl."

The doctor went on to point something out on the monitor, explaining how to tell the difference... but I was no longer hearing. My eyes were locked on the screen...

A little girl?

I couldn't quite explain it—how I couldn't take my eyes off her. I couldn't look away.

Knowing the gender made everything real, startlingly real. Everything felt fuzzy, blurred around the edges as I stared at my little one.

I might not have known about her a few hours ago, but now it was like my mind was glowing. Everything inside of me was warm and delighted and petrified... all while determination burned low in my gut. I was going to take care of her. My little girl was never going to have to go through the rejection I'd faced.

If I saw others treat her with the same cold indifference as what I'd faced at the Stonevalley castle, I would make them pay.

CHAPTER 25

MAGNUS

Three more hours passed before Dr. Lakeland checked all of Kira's vitals and cleared her to go.

Before releasing us, she gave Kira the same rundown that she'd gone over with me, listing out foods and activities that were recommended and which were forbidden.

My mate was clearly still tired, but gamely tried to listen to everything that the doctor went over. It was a lot of information, and some of it didn't even apply. The doctor said there was a slight risk from eating sushi. Where did she expect that we were going to get raw fish on the Stonevalley territory? Did the River wolves not have any idea how their neighboring packs lived? Our pack was highly isolated, within the heart of the forest, miles away from any humans. When were we going to have time to go to eat some sushi for lunch and endanger her pregnancy?

Once again, Erik Decoteau led us to the border of the River territory, though he was a lot less tense. He didn't even have a weapon pointed at us—not that he needed a bow and arrow to rip his enemies to shreds.

"There's a bridge three miles off the territory on the human land. It'll probably be safer." Erik nodded toward Kira's stomach.

Not that I knew Erik Decoteau well, but it was telling that he didn't even threaten to kill the pair of us a single time. For him, that was practically welcoming us into the pack with open arms if anything went wrong on our return.

But we would worry about that when we got to it.

"Give this message to your alpha," Erik Decoteau said, placing a sealed envelope in my hand. "At this point, I'll have to assume that our other attempt at reaching him wasn't effective."

"I'll make sure that the alpha's heir gets this," I said, taking the message.

Erik paused when I mentioned the Heir, watching me intently.

Our two packs didn't communicate. I hadn't heard of any official attempts of communication. Most of the information we had gathered about the River packs was through spying, and written reports from the generals.

He must not know about the alpha... his biological father.

I wasn't sure exactly what was going on, but our alpha hadn't been seen in public for years now. All I knew were the rumors that there were medical issues going on, and I wasn't about to repeat hearsay.

"The Heir makes decisions for our pack now," I brought up Aaron Ragnolf by title, not mentioning the fact that the two of them were brothers... The two hadn't seen one another in years. But it was more than years that separated them... the very treaty to end the war separated them.

Though the two shifters shared the same face, the same

womb, the same blood, they weren't brothers any longer in truth.

Erik didn't say a word.

I thought that was the end of his interest in the pack that had raised him, but after a pause, Erik asked, "How's Sofia?"

Sofia? The Heir's mate?

No. Sofia, the first-born daughter of the River pack alpha, who had been traded... for Erik.

She was just a year behind me in classes, though we had shared a single class. Back then, she had been quiet. A few of the idiots in the class messed with her—it never went beyond some childish name-calling. That never would have been tolerated, as physically harming her would have been in clear violation of the treaty between our packs. Of course, all bullying had ended when it was revealed to the pack that she was Aaron's soulmate.

"She's doing fine. I saw her a week ago, playing with her son," Kira answered, standing slightly behind me. "She seems happier now."

I couldn't blame Kira for feeling nervous. Any shifter could read the level of dominance radiating off the shifter in front of us. Kira was practically hiding her face behind my form, as if worried that Erik would somehow lose his perfect control and lash out at her.

For his part, Erik looked off into the distance, as if he were hesitating.

What more could he want to know?

There was no denying the loyalty that he showed to the River pack... the man seemed like he could rip out a Stonevalley wolf's throat and then cheerfully go home to eat a hearty breakfast of honey nut cheerios.

I couldn't give him any information that would put the

safety of the pack at risk. But then again, I did owe him my mate's life. He'd had her life in the palm of his hands and had shown her mercy.

There was nothing I could do to return the favor. He was owed a heavy debt. If it was in my power to answer his questions, there was no choice. I had to.

"Who is her mate?" Erik finally asked.

Erik really didn't know?

It hit me then, all the unfairness of the treaty... how it had ripped apart families and turned them into strangers. How it had forced children on to enemy territories, never to speak to one another again.

Erik didn't know that the shifter who had traded places with him was now the soulmate to his own brother.

I cleared my throat. If nothing else, Erik deserved to at least know the truth.

"Aaron Ragnolf," I said simply, saying the name of the alpha's heir. The man whom he'd once called brother.

Erik stared down in the direction of the Stonevalley pack without saying a word.

What would it feel like to learn that your own brother had something as life changing as a soulbond? Did it do anything other than highlight the distance between the two of them?

He nodded to us in goodbye before turning back to his territory and leaving us behind.

Kira was silent as we traveled back to the territory of the Stone wolves. The surrounding air was flooded with the chemical stench of cortisol. She had her arms crossed tightly across her chest, staring down hard at the ground.

No. My mate wasn't going to trudge listlessly back to her territory with her tail between her legs like a beaten dog.

I wrapped my arms around her shoulders, halting her, and leaning close to the shell of her ear to whisper. "We don't have to go back if you don't want to."

Kira shook her head. "I want to go back, I just can't stop thinking that if I never ran in the first place, then we wouldn't have to worry about getting kicked out of our pack."

"I'm not surprised you ran. I was an asshole and never apologized."

From the first moment that I realized Kira was my mate, I'd braced for her to run. I knew exactly the lengths I had gone to push her away.

"What if I ruined everything?" her voice got small as she looked into the distance, blinking to force herself not to cry.

I linked my hands with hers. "You haven't ruined anything." Nothing between us was ruined. Everything between us was just beginning.

"But what if we can't be together in the Stonevalley pack? What if I got us thrown out after all the work that you've done? You've become one of the youngest generals in a century. I can't let you throw that all away because I did something stupid."

I shook my head.

Being a general, all of my rank and status in the pack— none of that mattered. None of that had ever made me happy. I had always felt something grating at me... something glaringly missing. I hadn't started feeling right and whole until the moment that I sank into Kira's tight pussy for the first time.

She had no idea... didn't understand at all... none of it mattered without *her*.

But then again, why would she know that? I had never bothered to let her know. Now my mate was kicking herself for reacting to the shitty way *I'd* treated her. If I had only been honest with her from the very beginning about how much I wanted her... how much my life had always revolved around her... she would have never had a cause to run.

That miscommunication ended now.

"You're mine. There's no place you could run to, where I couldn't find you." Even if she ran again, it wouldn't matter. I would be right behind her, tracking her footsteps until the moment we were together again.

I leaned in closer, kissing a heated trail from her shoulders, across her slender neck, all the way to the plush curves of her lips. "I'd follow you anywhere."

CHAPTER 26
KIRA

It was dark by the time Magnus and I reached the Stonevalley castle.

I'd automatically started to head around to the stables, planning to sneak in through one of the side passages, but Magnus took my hand in his and led us through the grand front entrance.

When I glanced up at him questioningly, Magnus shrugged and said, "We've been gone for three days, and I've abandoned my post. There's no hiding what we've done. Might as well face it head on."

I hadn't entered the Stonevalley castle this way in years. The high stone archways, the heavy portcullis, it all made me feel small. I swallowed as the guards on duty raised the grid of metal bars, allowing us into the castle. Neither of the shifters on duty said a word to us, but I felt their eyes on our backs as we stepped through into the Great Hall.

Inside the castle, all was quiet. Though I somehow expected that the alpha's heir himself would somehow sense our wrong doing, and come to challenge Magnus. The

Heir's shifter form was a monster more than a wolf. He could shred us to pieces in moments for our crimes.

None of that happened, though. No one said a word to either of us as Magnus led me through grand carpeted stairways, passing by gilded portraits of the former alphas and warriors in all of their military regalia.

Magnus didn't loosen his grip on my hand until he'd led me all the way inside of his room. There, surrounded by the thick aroma that was musky spice, delicious, and all *him.*

Once back in his room, Magnus relaxed, sitting down to tear off his boots.

I bit my lip, watching him undress.

Now that the two of us were back home and here in this space that was all his... I couldn't help suddenly feeling like the tentative closeness that had grown between us out in the River territory had dried up.

His room was so much grander than mine. I could fit half of my room just in his closet. The fact that he had his own personal bathroom and a tub with gilded lion paws... I'd never felt my low status in the pack so keenly before.

I didn't belong here.

As Magnus changed, I quietly stepped toward the door. My dingy room was small, and I might share a hallway bathroom with half a dozen others, but it was infinitely safer.

I only got a handful of steps before Magnus placed his hand on my shoulder, stopping me... beneath the thin fabric of my shirt, my soulmark lit up in response to his touch.

Magnus' voice deepened, husky and demanding. "Stay with me."

"I thought..." I don't actually know what I thought. I sort of just panicked. "You never invited me to stay before."

"I always want you to stay." Magnus tugged me back until I was flush against his chest, holding me tight against him. "You're mine. You belong with me. In my bed and under me. I want you by my side as you grow my child. I never want to be parted from you."

Magnus scooped me up in his arms, holding me like I didn't weigh a thing. He carried me across his room to his bed, dropping me on top of silky-smooth sheets. Then he followed me down, pressing his half undressed body on top of mine. I could feel the heat of his skin searing me through my clothes. Lighting me on fire.

"If you need an invitation, here it is. I want you in my bed. Every night. Starting right now." Then he pressed his plush lips to mine, kissing me deeply, like he wanted to inhale all of me.

My head started to swirl with all the delicious sensations as Magnus pressed me harder into his bed. His tongue stroked across mine with a slick friction that tasted sweeter than sin.

He tasted like crisp apples and desire... he tasted like he was mine.

His knee pressed between my thighs, roughly parting them. Magnus watched me with naked want within stormy gray eyes.

"I'm not letting you get away from me." he pressed searing open-mouthed kisses against my neck. "If I have to, I'll fuck you until you can't walk away."

I could feel him hard against my inner thigh. Every single muscular inch of him rested on top of me. He was built like a tank, with his big body pressed firmly against me until I couldn't move an inch.

Magnus wasted no time pulling every last stitch of clothing off my body and his, shredding the fabric that he couldn't get off fast enough. The way that his touches bit in a little too roughly as he positioned me where he wanted me, spreading my legs wider... the way that he clutched my hips, grinding against me—with every touch it was more and more clear.

Magnus *wanted* me.

All the unyielding strength in his powerful body...

My lower belly heated with pure unadulterated want, as Magnus caressed my hips and stroked along my sides, leaving trails of desire across my skin.

Too soon I was a mess, dripping for him. My entire body was alight, burning with need. The only thing that I could feel was an aching emptiness. I needed him to fill it.

My eyes fluttered closed, as I was lost to everything but my soulmate's touches, the press of his mouth, and his solid presence above me.

He stopped moving, denying me the pleasure I desperately needed. Without having to say it, I knew what he was doing. What he was waiting for.

Eyes on me.

Magnus wouldn't give me any of that delicious friction that my body was craving. Not until I acknowledged *exactly* from whom my pleasure came.

My eyes snapped open, and immediately locked on to the storm brewing in his eyes. I was drawn into the hunger in his gaze. He was looking at me like I was the most exquisite meal, and he was ready to devour me. Bite by bite.

Gazing at him, the thought struck me with all the force of lightning. Yes, Magnus might have been the face of the man who'd bullied me growing up... who could eviscerate with a cruel word just as effectively as ripping apart his enemies... but that wasn't how I saw him anymore. This handsome, possessive and deadly man. He was *mine*.

I reached up, cupping his jaw in the palm of my hand, feeling the intoxicating heat of his skin. The rough prickling of his five-o'clock shadow.

"I'm not running away." I parted my legs wider for him, needing him closer. I wanted him deep within my body, in the same way that I had made room for him somewhere deep within my very soul. "I'm right where I want to be."

His pupils darkened, as Magnus lost the last grip he had on his control.

Magnus notched the fat head of his cock right at my entrance. With one sharp thrust he entered me.

The way that his hips jerked against mine... the way that I could feel every inch of his girth dragging across my walls as he pulled almost all the way out, before thrusting sharply inside once more—it was rough, almost frantic, and exactly how I wanted it.

He was everything. Every sensation narrowed down to just him—his touches, his kisses, and his harsh strokes deep within me.

He was the only thing I could feel and everything I'd ever need.

Maybe it was because I had finally admitted that I wanted him, or maybe it was because he'd already vowed to fuck me until I couldn't walk... Whatever the reason, the sex between us felt different. Raw and primal. Magnus slammed inside of me with brutal thrusts that were so powerful that each harsh stroke shifted me up the bed. Over and over, until I was right up against the headboard.

Magnus' eyes were locked on my body, fixed on the point where the two of us connected; watching me take his big cock again and again.

His gaze was more than possessive. It was utterly *searing*.

It was all so much.

The way Magnus was fucking me like he never wanted to stop, the way that he stared at my body as he claimed me as his...

Suddenly, without warning, my orgasm erupted through me.

Molten pleasure pulsed through my core, sending lightning down my spine. I cried out as my walls squeezed Magnus cock tight. Waves of pleasure rushed through me, strong enough to knock me down if I wasn't already flat on my back.

"That's it," he praised me. "Milk my cock, Baby."

He kissed my lips sweetly, as aftershocks coursed down my limbs like electricity.

By the time my orgasm had run its course, I was about ready to melt straight into the bed.

But my soulmate wasn't done with me.

Magnus lifted my legs over his shoulder, giving himself better access. Then he began to move, pounding into me fast and hard.

I moaned helplessly, unable to do anything but take him, as he proved with each slam of his cock how this pussy was his.

His thrusts were savage, as he slammed into me deep, until it was impossible to tell where he stopped and I began. He was thrusting deep enough within me to erase all of the distance and the hurt... maybe even hard enough to break through all the mistakes we'd made in the past.

With a groan that was masculine and thoroughly satisfied, Magnus came. His hips jerked against mine, as he pushed in deep, flooding me with his cum.

He braced himself over me, biceps shaking as he caught his breath. Though he withdrew himself from me gently, my mate didn't move far. Magnus wrapped my arms around me, as if physically reminding me of my promise to stay.

But I was so tired. My eyelids had never been heavier, as I sunk into his warm embrace, and the safety of his arms around me.

He felt like home.

CHAPTER 27
KIRA

The warmest, most comfortable sleep I ever had was rudely interrupted by harsh banging. I fought against waking, snuggling harder against the most perfect warmth... until my pillow stirred from beneath me.

What the? What was...

Everything came back to me in a rush—my panic fueled escape from the Stonevalley territory, my run in with the vampire... how Magnus had rescued me and all the promises we had whispered to each other in the dark since then.

Instead of the panic I'd anticipated from being in Magnus' bed, in his room... waking up in his *arms*... all I felt was a grumpy dissatisfaction at getting woken up at stupid-o-clock in the morning.

"The fuck?" Magnus grumbled, only half awake.

He pressed a groggy kiss to my forehead as he disentangled himself from me, taking all of his delicious heat with him as he stumbled out of bed.

I opened up one eye, squinting against the early

morning light as I watched my mate pull on a pair of pants and stride across the room to his door. My gaze lingered on the sculpted muscles of his back. If this wasn't too important, maybe there would be time to continue where we'd left off last night...

Magnus jerked the door open to reveal the panicked face of my brother, Sylas.

I rolled my eyes.

As soon as I saw it was Sylas at the door, I pulled the covers straight over my head,

shutting out all the light and tugging the blankets tighter against me to reclaim some of the cozy warmth I'd lost.

I love my brother, I really do... but couldn't he wait for the sun to fully rise before coming to see whether or not I was alive?

I did my best to ignore their hushed conversation, closing my eyes and inviting back sleep. Even got halfway there, when a familiar hand brushed along my shoulder, gently waking me.

Reluctantly, I emerged out of the comfortable blankets. Magnus was watching me, with the hint of a smile tugging at the corner of his mouth.

"Here," he handed me some of his clothes that were definitely not going to fit me, "your brother wants to check on you."

"Tell him to go," I grumbled, ignoring the clothes.

Magnus shook his head, "I'm going to report to the Heir. Stay close to Sylas until I come back."

Well, that woke me up.

I shrugged into Magnus' clothes. His shirt fell down to my mid-thighs and I had to roll the band of his sweatpants three times before they would stay on my body.

Magnus watched me get changed with an expression suggesting that he would be happier to tear his clothes back off me, if he didn't have to go take care of business.

"What if the Heir exiles us?" My voice was a whisper, as if saying the words softly could stop them from coming true.

"I'm pretty sure the River pack would take us. Or we could try Evenfall Ridge or the Blackwood pack," Magnus shrugged.

"Right." My gaze fell down to my hands in my lap, as something deep in my stomach was sinking.

"Hey," Magnus gently held my cheek in his hands. "As long as we're together, it doesn't matter to me."

He pressed another kiss to my forehead, then strode out of the room. Off to handle the consequences of my mistakes.

Now I had to deal with my brother. Even from under the blankets, the clear scent of anger and panic radiated off him. But I was so tired. Soothing my brother's feelings was almost more than I could handle when I had my own anxiety to deal with.

The moment that I opened the door for him, Sylas burst in like he owned the place.

"Where the fuck have you been?" Sylas didn't even give me a chance to answer before he pulled me close for a hug. "I was so worried about you."

My annoyance melted, when I felt how tightly he held me. I completely understood. I was his only sibling and I'd disappeared for days without a word. In his shoes, I'd be pissed off at me too.

He had probably been imagining that the worst kinds of things happened to me... and unfortunately, I was about to prove that he was right to have imagined it.

"I ran away... to unclaimed territory." I winced as his expression immediately soured as Sylas went into full-blown overprotective older brother mode.

"What the hell were you thinking? Do you have any idea how dangerous that is?" My brother looked just about ready to kill me for daring to do something so stupid I almost died.

"Well, now I do. I got attacked by a vampire." I muttered.

"What?!" His voice had never gotten so high-pitched before in his entire life. He stared at me to see if I was joking, and cursed when he realized it was all too real. "So did you fight it off? Did your wolf go for the neck?"

"Actually, no. It bit me. Almost sucked me dry." My cheeks flushed with heat.

Sylas' face paled, as he leaned in closer and stared blatantly at my neck, looking for the bite mark.

"Damn it, Kira." Sylas' eyes were wide with panic. "Are you going to... to turn?"

Sylas clenched his hands so hard that his knuckles were white.

I shook my head.

At the very least the doctor reassured me that I wouldn't become a blood sucking monster.

Oh shit... the doctor. The *River* doctor. The one that I had to abandon the pack for, traveling to enemy territory without the alpha's permission... because if I hadn't the blood loss might have killed me.

"Magnus came in time. He killed it... it's just that he had to take me to the Edgeriver pack to get treated. I don't know how the Heir is going to react at all." It was well within the Heir's right to exile Magnus and I from the pack for abandoning our duties, for trespassing straight on enemy territory.

Technically, there was a treaty in place between our packs —a treaty that did nothing to erase the blood already spilled between the Stone and River wolves. A decade ago, traveling to the River pack would have resulted in an automatic banishment. Now, I had no idea how the alpha's heir would react.

"Goddess. Why the hell did you run away?" Sylas was running his hands through his hair, looking like he was right on the verge of ripping it straight out. Then suddenly his eyes darkened, as he leaned closer to me, asking in a quiet voice, "Did Magnus do anything to you?"

Yeah.

My brother was right in guessing that Magnus did something.

But the awful thing that Magnus had said that put me into a full blown panic... was to tell me that he loves me.

Which for some reason a few days ago was the most horrible thing that he could have possibly said to me.

"No, I wasn't thinking. I just panicked... Magnus wouldn't do anything to me." Because Magnus *loves* me.

My cheeks burned even hotter when I realized that what I'd told Sylas wasn't even the most shocking news

"But," my voice trailed off. "That isn't all." I had barely come to terms with the change that was happening in my own body, and now I was going to have to tell Sylas... it was basically physical proof I was having sex. I mean, Sylas already knew, but that didn't mean that I wanted to shove the evidence right under his nose.

There was no going around it. If I got banished, and torn away from my brother, never able to see Sylas anymore, I wanted him to know.

"You were only gone for a few days." Sylas muttered, darkly. "How did you manage to get into this much trouble? What else could have possibly happened?"

I wrung my hands as my mind raced. What was the least embarrassing way to tell him? Do I say that there's a bun in the oven? Do I just tell him?

"You're going to be an uncle." I said in a rush, before hiding my face in my hands so I wouldn't have to see his reaction.

In silence, I waited for him to say anything. After a moment, I peeked out a glance at him from between my fingers.

"What's that supposed to mean?"

His face was totally blank.

Goddess, help me. I was going to have to explain it to him.

"I'm going to have a baby."

Sylas eyebrow shot up so high it practically disappeared into his hairline. He shot a dubious glance at my very flat stomach.

Why was it so hard to think that I could be pregnant? He had known that Magnus and I were... umm... intimate.

"The doctor said that she's measuring at three months already. Honestly, I'm surprised that you hadn't noticed." So much for his heightened wolf senses.

"I wasn't trying to notice your scent. The opposite, actually."

I didn't think that my face could burn any hotter until I realized *why* Sylas was actively trying to avoid my scent. That meant that all this time, he was able to sniff it out and know every time that Magnus and I engaged in certain *activities.*

"This isn't a joke? You're really pregnant?"

"Yes!" I snapped, my frustration was boiling over.

"Okay, calm down. I'm going to go see if Magnus keeps any wine in his room." Sylas turned, on the verge of hunting down some alcohol—one thing the doctor vehemently told me I could not have for the next seven months or so.

"I can't drink wine!" I was just about ready to tear my hair out in frustration. Why did I think my brother would be a good support for this? What exactly did he know about women's bodies and pregnancy?

Sylas frowned. "Well then, how are we going to celebrate?"

"Celebrate?"

I frowned right back at him.

What was he talking about? My mate was off to talk with the alpha's heir about the huge mess I made. If we were exiled, I might not ever see my brother again.

"I mean, you're going to have a baby." Sylas said each word slowly, letting the message really sink in. "The two of us are going to celebrate."

I placed my hand over my stomach.

After the very dramatic way I'd found out about the baby in my belly, I didn't have the headspace to really think about her. Besides my fierce drive to protect her, it all seemed so new.

I didn't have time to be happy about her.

"How could you even think about celebrating right now? If I get kicked out of the pack in the next hour or so, I might never see you again."

Sylas snorted like *I* was being the ridiculous one.

"That's not happening." Sylas crossed his hands over his chest like he had any say in this.

"What?"

Sylas shook his head. "I'm not leaving you. If you get kicked out, I'm coming with you."

My jaw dropped in shock.

But he. Sylas... He couldn't just do that.

He'd worked so hard for so many years, climbing all the way up the social ladder. I couldn't let him throw that all away.

"But—"

"Don't even try to talk me out of it. You think I'd abandon my little sister? That I'm going to let my niece grow up without her favorite uncle? Fuck that. Absolutely not."

My chin wouldn't stop wobbling as my eyes stung. I blinked hard to hold back tears, torn between thanking him and letting Sylas know that he was officially the world's biggest idiot.

"Now help me find something bubbly in here that's not wine. You're going to have a baby, and we're going to celebrate."

CHAPTER 28

KIRA

"So I'm assuming things are better between you and Magnus now?" Sylas had popped open a bottle of sparkling apple juice and handed me a glass.

I took a sip, letting the bubbles fizzle on my tongue, letting them distract me from thoughts of Magnus facing down an enraged Heir.

Shifters were highly territorial. There was no guarantee that we would be allowed back. Wolves depended on one another for their survival. We worked together to defend our land, providing protection through our numbers and our bonds of loyalty.

It was worse for Magnus, as he had a position of authority in the pack. As a general, Magnus commanded other shifters in times of war. Under the alpha's authority, he would be responsible for making the right decisions for our pack, leading the others.

What if the Heir saw Magnus' actions as a betrayal?

Goddess, what if he got hurt?

All Magnus had ever done was protect me. Even now he was protecting me. He was facing the most dominant wolf in our pack alone, while I hid in his room drinking his apple juice.

Magnus might have been taking the blame for this, but he was wrong. I had let myself get too caught up in our past to see him clearly.

I was the one who was judging him for months based on who *was*.

And if I hadn't done all that? If I hadn't been blinded by the past, how would I have seen him now?

Would I have seen a man that had always showed up whenever I needed him?

Would I have acknowledged that he was always kind to me, always treated me as nothing less than a queen?

Would I have admitted in my scared little heart that the reason I craved him... it went deeper than attraction.

No matter how loudly I tried to deny it... deep within me, I knew that being with him made me feel whole.

Oh, *shit*.

This burning hope for his safety—from my whole heart, and strength and soul... I knew what it meant.

I still hadn't answered my brother.

I nodded slowly. My voice stuck in my throat, weighed down by the heavy revelation.

"I love him."

I just had to pray to the goddess that I didn't realize it too late.

CHAPTER 29
MAGNUS

On an executive desk with gold in-lay and black borders, lay a neat stack of paperwork. The man sitting behind the desk appeared focused and calm, but his scent was acidic with anger.

Aaron Ragnolf didn't look up from his work as he read his morning reports. With a heavy sigh, he scrawled his signature across the page, placing it neatly in a new stack.

No other shifter I'd ever met matched the dominance brimming in the Heir. It was possible that he was the most powerful shifter on the continent, if not in the entire world. Before I'd met Erik Decoteau, I'd never imagined that anyone could come close to his power.

Being in the pack intensified his authority. Aaron Ragnolf was my alpha. His dominance ruled over the territory, and bound me to it.

Dominance that I had blatantly defied in my mad rush to save Kira.

Kira.

My thoughts drifted to her soft curls. The depths of her ocean blue eyes.

I'd do it again.

I'd bared my throat on River territory, offering a clean shot if it gave my mate a chance to live. Now that I returned, I was essentially doing the same here.

I would never regret saving her.

Never.

Then eyes that were blue and piercing locked on me.

"You abandoned your post." Aaron Ragnolf said, laying out the facts of my mad rush to rescue Kira bare and out in the open. "In fact, you caused panic throughout the castle. I had several inquiries about whether we were under attack."

Right. One would think that in a castle filled with people that could break apart their bodies and transform into full-fledged beasts, that the sight of our wolves wouldn't be enough to start a panic.

However, the Stonevalley fighting wolves were highly disciplined. It wasn't often that one of the shifters lost control.

Everyone must have assumed the worst—that some unknown enemy had already made their way through the castle gates.

Wolves didn't run through the ornate gilded hallways of the Stonevalley castle for no reason. People reacted to my wolf with real fear.

Aaron Ragnolf leaned closer. "The last general who deserted the Stonevalley wolves was hunted down about two centuries ago. My father had his head displayed on the battlement."

I held myself perfectly still.

I might be a strong wolf. In class, some of my teachers had called me a prodigy. But Aaron Ragnolf was born with a level of raw power that seemed supernatural.

If the outcome of this meeting came down to a fight

between me and the alpha's heir, it was obvious who was stronger and who would be ripped to shreds. My wolf was a puppy compared to the absolute beast hidden within Aaron Ragnolf's body.

"I gave you this position. I hand picked you as one of my generals. You have performed admirably. Until now."

Aaron Ragnolf would not be lenient. Carefully I grabbed hold of my emotions, forcing myself to be calm—I had to, if I wanted any chance of making it out of this office alive.

"At this point, you would be lucky to lose your rank and status. Give me one good reason why I shouldn't put you in an early grave."

There was no excuse for my behavior. All I could do was tell him the truth and face justice for my actions.

I raised my bare palm, showing the Heir the soulmark burned into my skin.

"I could feel my soulmate getting attacked." There was no excuse for what I had done. Yet, I doubt any other shifter who could feel their mate's pain would act differently. "I have no desire to abandon my duties, but I had to save her. She would have died without medical intervention."

Aaron Ragnolf cocked his head in a wolfish gesture, piercing me with the intense pressure of his full attention; like a predator holding all the power of his body at bay, readying himself for the kill.

He watched me as if for the first time he could completely see me.

"I should have suspected as much, as soon as I heard that one of my young generals went off the rails, that it had to be something like this." Aaron Ragnolf's stoic expression did not change, but the scent of anger faded.

Did this mean that I was off the hook? Without moving

an inch, I stood at attention, waiting for the Heir to decide what he was going to do with me.

"You said that you were gone for three days for a medical intervention." There was a flicker of concern in his eyes. "Did you have to take your soulmate to the Edgeriver pack?"

"Yes, they were able to heal her." I pulled from my pocket the ultrasound picture, placing it on the alpha heir's desk. "She's pregnant, about three months along. It's why she wasn't able to shift and protect herself."

The Heir blinked in surprise. "How long have the two of you been mated?"

"Our soulbond sparked at the Masked Ball." I admitted.

Aaron Ragnolf gave me a look that said that he could do the mental math, and he *knew* that Ball was only three months ago. Even the Alpha's Heir realized that I knocked up my mate right away.

"I can't fault you for saving your mate, but I can't ignore the fact that your stunt disrupted the peace in the castle." Aaron Ragnolf's nostrils flared, taking in my scent. Checking for signs that I was a coward. That I was nothing but a disgraceful punk that didn't deserve the responsibilities of my position.

I gave him none.

Aaron Ragnolf nodded, his perusal of me complete. "You're on desk duty. I'm going to put you to work filing old records."

It was grunt work, and boring—though it would keep me inside the castle, close to my pregnant mate. The mate who wouldn't have to be ripped away from everything that she knew here.

Relief coursed through me. All the tight pressure across my shoulders, keeping me rigid and tense, began to unwind. I felt light, as a weight I didn't know I was holding was released.

Wait.

Speaking of important paperwork…

"There's one more thing." I handed the sealed letter, though now it was folded and crumpled at the edges from journeying across miles of forest in my pocket. "This is a message from the Edgeriver pack."

The alpha's heir froze. Claws burst neatly through one finger as he sliced through the wax seal.

"This is from Erik…" Aaron Ragnolf said out loud, as his eyes quickly darted across the letter. After a moment, he slowly laid the letter down on his desk. "When you were there, did you notice any evidence of silver sickness?"

I nodded in the affirmative. "The scent of silver was all over their infirmary, and several of the patient's rooms were labeled with it."

Aaron Ragnolf sighed heavily, placing the Edgeriver message right on top of the stack of paperwork he'd already gone through. Whatever the message said, it was yet one more thing for him to deal with. The alpha's heir met my eyes, nodding to me in a clear dismissal.

I bowed my head in deference.

Halfway out of his office, Aaron Ragnolf called out to me.

"Tell your mate to wear her best at dinner tonight. We're going to have a feast."

I turned back, quickly wiping the shock off my face. When I looked back at the Heir, he was smiling.

"The Goddess has finally blessed our pack with another child."

CHAPTER 30
MAGNUS

I wanted to sprint back to her... only the Heir's warning about the chaos I'd already caused held me back. I walked back to my mate in a daze, letting the adrenaline fade. Letting the message that we weren't exiled sink in.

I opened the door to my room, to find Kira and Sylas laughing, an open bottle of sweet and fizzy apple juice between them.

Kira's look turned serious the moment that she saw me. My little mate jumped to her feet and rushed over to me.

"How did things go with the Heir?" Her voice was tense as she scanned my expression for a hint of how the rest of her future would unfold.

I could imagine the questions that must be swirling around in her lovely head—did we need to start packing? Were we about to make the long trek out into our uncertain new roles in brand new packs?

"We need to get ready." I said, grabbing a stray lock of Kira's curly hair and placing it gently behind her ear.

Kira's face fell as she nodded.

I smiled. "Because the Heir is throwing us a banquet."

My soulmate was staring at me like I had grown a second head.

I was already picturing the dress that I was going to order for her. If we moved fast, and got all of her measurements in time, the tailor would be able to put something together for her tonight—I was looking forward to finally seeing Kira in a dress that was worthy of her.

I leaned down, my fingers skimming along Kira's trim lower belly. "He wants to welcome our little one into the pack."

Sylas was shaking his head, muttering something about how of course I broke the rules and then somehow got a feast out of it.

I didn't bother to reply.

I only had eyes for Kira.

Her voice was a whisper as she asked, "does that mean we really get to stay?"

I don't think that I ever smiled wider, as I nodded to my little mate.

All of a sudden, Kira wrapped her arms around me, pulling me in a tight hug. She squeezed me hard, burrowing her adorable little face into my chest.

"I love you," she whispered.

Even with her face pressed tight against me, I heard every word.

Every muscle in my body froze. I stared at Kira in utter shock.

The girl I'd wanted for most of life. The mother of my child... my soulmate.

She loves me?

I pulled her to me, dragging her so close that her feet lifted off the floor, as my lips crashed into hers.

Pressing her soft curves against me, slipping my hand under the hem of her shirt, to feel the warmth of her skin.

I had to taste her, had to feel her... the girl who *loves* me.

Before I even had the opportunity to growl at Sylas to get the fuck out, I heard the slam of the door as he made a hasty exit.

Hopefully, we might get lucky enough to find a dress that was already her size.

We weren't going to make it to the tailor.

Kira wore a silk and velvet dress in a shade of blue that was an exact match for her eyes. Her drop-waist ball gown showed off all the lovely curves in her hourglass figure, while the crystal applique in the bodice drew in the eye. The cut of the dress dipped low enough to show off a tiny hint of the world's loveliest breasts. Her shoulders were bare, exposing her soulmark to the eyes of the entire pack for the first time ever.

Kira clutched my arm as I walked her into the dining hall. All eyes were on us as we entered together. Some of the other shifters were openly pointing at the cluster of constellations that marked her soulbond, and the obviously matching one on my bare palm.

If I'd seen her wearing this before, I would have ripped the head off any male that dared to look at her for a moment too long.

Now, I barely had the urge to kill every single man in the room.

No.

Not anymore, when it was so obvious that Kira was my soulmate.

Nothing but pride surged through me, even as all males in the pack gaped at her. Let them look, and see exactly what they would never have. Kira was *mine*. Not only had the moon goddess written the soulmark into her skin, showing everyone the connection between us...

Kira had admitted it herself.

She *loves* me.

I have no idea what it was that I'd done. I don't think I even did enough to have earned her forgiveness. But it didn't matter. Kira wanted me and she would have me.

I'd prove to her every moment for the rest of her life that she had made the right decision.

As soon as we got to the high table, my gorgeous girl blushed furiously as I pulled out a chair for her. She was seated in a place of honor, directly to the right of the Heir and his family.

Even Sylas was around from wherever he usually took his meals. It was odd that he'd never eaten with higher ranking wolves, no matter how his status climbed in the pack. Now he took a seat across from his sister with a wink.

My soulmate's blush turned even deeper as the Heir led the entire pack in a toast to her, congratulating our soul-bond and her pregnancy.

She was right where she belonged, in a place of honor and by my side.

Finally, *finally,* everyone could look at Kira Valdis and acknowledge the truth—the truth that I had felt from the moment I first laid my eyes on her.

That she was *mine*. That she was made for me.

Nothing could be better than this.

CHAPTER 31

KIRA

SEVEN MONTHS LATER

I waited for months for my belly to get bigger, for it to look like I was actually going to have a child.

It almost felt like I was lying for attention about the whole pregnancy.

Obviously, I could feel my daughter kicking. I knew that she was there... but month after month, I never noticed a baby bump.

At least the shifter wolves could scent the change in my pheromones. I could have told any of the humans in the pack that I just ate a little too much at the banquet and they would never have even suspected that I was nearly about to deliver a baby.

I swear she was still in there.

Magnus and I had even gotten written permission to travel over to the Edgeriver doctor to check on the little girl's health.

The doctor said that the small belly wasn't a concern at all. She mentioned something about my stomach muscles being very strong, and that my torso was long, so my womb was growing up instead of pushing out.

All of her measurements and vital signs looked normal. In fact, Dr. Lakeland said that her head was pointed down and I should be ready to deliver at any time. She had actually asked me if I wanted to stick around for a few days.

I wanted to have my baby born in Stonevalley territory. I wasn't about to give anyone any reason why my baby should be treated like an outsider. If she was going to be raised in these castle walls, then she'd be born inside of them.

The doctor told me that if she wasn't needed so desperately by some of her other patients, she would have trekked across the forest that separated our territories to help me deliver my daughter.

But I was confident in myself. I might not have access to the medical equipment at the River territory, but it wasn't like I had any complications to worry about. My little one looked healthy and—

A small burst of pressure tightened across my hips and lower abdomen.

What was that? What *was* that?

I sat down on the comfy rocking chair that Magnus had insisted on getting for me, gripping the arms of the chair so hard that I must be etching nail marks into the wood.

Magnus burst into the room, practically ripping the door from its hinges. The look on his face was more panicked than I'd ever seen him. Then it all clicked.

Oh.

Right.

I was going into labor.

SHE LOOKED UP AT ME, with her wrinkly little face, confusion in her blue-gray eyes, as if she didn't know why I had rudely evicted her from her last comfy home.

She had a full head of hair that was curly and just a shade darker than my honey-brown. Her little features were tiny and pixie-like.

My little girl was *perfect*.

"Obviously, we're naming her Magna, after me." Magnus held out a finger to her chubby clenched fists, trying to coax her to reach out and grab onto his finger.

I'd already vowed to make sure that my daughter could live a life without being scorned and ostracized. There was no way that I was naming her something so awful that it put a huge bullying target on her back.

I gave him a *look*, silently communicating that if he ever wanted more babymaking, he had to start taking her name seriously. Immediately.

Magnus cleared his throat.

"Maggie, after me."

My eyes narrowed at him. I was not naming my child something that sounded like a nickname.

"Or we could combine our names and name her Mira?"

I was too tired to ask who told him that combination names were a good idea. Luckily, Magnus picked up on my distaste for the name and went quiet in thought.

"What about Mia?"

She *did* look like a Mia.

It was another combination name, but somehow this one didn't strike me as a bad idea.

"Mia."

The name was sweet and lovely and rolled off the tongue. As soon as I said the name out loud, I knew that it was hers.

It reminded me of us. How at first I thought that we could never work. We were too different, too volatile. Kira Valdis and Magnus Grimson? Before the soulbond, nothing would have convinced me that the two of us could ever be a good idea.

But somehow, when we came together, everything fell perfectly into place.

Also by Miyo Hunter

Moonlight Reborn

He was the most dominant wolf in the pack and I'm the bullied outcast he hates until his skin touched mine, electricity sparked. Marking us. We both knew what it meant—a soulbond.

Moonlight Shifter

Finding your soulmate is every wolf shifter's dream—except mine. I'm already in love. So when destiny revealed my mate, I did the only thing I could. I ran from him. But no matter how strong I am, a lone wolf is vulnerable. When I'm captured, the only one who can come for me, is the mate I'd rejected.

His Gold Pack Omega

A shattered omega socialite, rejected by society.

After what I went through, becoming an outcast was the only way to survive. But now none of the laws protecting omegas apply to me.

I hired him to be my bodyguard. He's all raw strength, gorgeous and protective.I feel drawn to him, and the heat in his gaze makes me feel alive again. For the first time in years, I feel safe. But how can I let him in without letting him see the broken thing I've become?

*Knot Your Basic B*tch*

Who wants a shot at love and a pack of their very own? Not this b*tch.

Nothing will stand between me and my dream—to finally get a

nice calm secretarial job—not even sexy twins or chiseled abs. At least, that's what I tell myself.

But when destiny crashes into all my careful plans with HOT scent matches, will I be able to cling to my hope for a simple life? Or will I let them sweep me off my feet?

About the Author

I'm Miyo Hunter and I'm addicted to Dominant Alphas. Sweet love and dark fantasy. From shifters to omegaverse, I want characters bent over chairs and called a good girl. I want to read until jobs and responsibilities don't exist. Until I'm lost in a world that's spicy and a little bit wild.

instagram.com/miyohunter

tiktok.com/@miyohunter